Leading Man

Hollywood to Olympus, Book 3

Elle Rush

Published 2015

Cover design by Lyn Taylor
Formatted by Self-Publishing Services LLC. (www.Self-
Publishing-Service.com)

ISBN: 978-0-9939904-2-7

Blurb

Olympus heartthrob Nick Thurston is a leading man with a problem. His new play opens in a month and when it comes to the pivotal waltz scene, he can't lead. When he broke up with his dance instructor girlfriend, it also ended their professional relationship and now he needs a new teacher. Desperately.

Ashleigh Jessup needs to find a new building to take her booming dance studio to the next level. She doesn't have time for a private student, but she's willing to make an exception to do a favor for a friend and earn extra money for her down payment.

Ashleigh's success has come at the cost of her love life, so she can't believe it when Nick is good with them spending as much time on their careers as they do with each other. But when Nick's ex tries to sabotage their relationship, Nick begins to doubt Ashleigh's intentions when she benefits from his fame, and Ashleigh has to decide if she's willing to risk her business for a relationship Nick may not even believe in.

Dedication

Special thanks to all my Chat girls.

Chapter 1

"Naked is better." Nick Thurston was deadly serious in his declaration. "I would rather have a scene with full-frontal nudity on an outdoor stage in January in Alaska than go to one more dance class with that—" Damn his parents for teaching him not to curse when referring to a lady, although the lady in question didn't meet the moral definition of one.

"Woman," his salt-and-pepper haired lawyer suggested.

"She is not a woman. She's some kind of handsy, tap-dancing nightmare. The world may know I have two left feet but I swear she has at least four arms because one of them is pinching my ass while the other is picking my pocket." He glanced over at the man who had shepherded both him and his parents from their first-roles to superstardom and was not impressed to find him laughing. "Brian, I mean it. This isn't a little mutually fun flirting. It's sexual harassment and regular harassment and I am done with it."

"Nick, I believe you."

"Then fix it. I'm one of the producers for 'The Last Bachelor.' I should have the ability to fire her for harassment, shouldn't I? At this point I'd be willing to buy out her contract in order to be rid of her and take the financial hit to replace her. Find me a loophole, please. Or some Kevlar slacks if you can't—my backside is one big bruise." Nick ran his hands through his lightly gelled hair, which reminded him he needed to refresh the sun-streaked blond highlights he added for the summer. He leaned against the bookshelf along the wall. He winced and stood up straight again. He wasn't kidding about the bruise.

As much as he griped, Nick wasn't certain there was much the man could do. Brian had done his best to talk Nick out of hiring his then-girlfriend Sandrine Gold as their choreographer, insisting Nick had enough on his plate with his role and financial contribution in the production. Nick brushed aside Brian's concerns, insisting he wanted to be involved in all aspects of the play, including hiring the stage hands and specialists. He wasn't going to miss any part of the next phase of his career.

Nick loved playing Ares on Olympus and was thrilled the hit drama was heading into its fourth season. The Spartactus/Game of Thrones/Hercules mash-up was a lot of work and a lot of fun and he wouldn't trade it for the world but the simple truth was he wanted a change from togas. The hiatus after the show's thirteen-episode third season offered him the perfect opportunity to try something new. In this case, Colby Sinclair, one of his former co-stars from his Paradise Point days, had moved into directing and had called Nick with the offer of a lifetime—the title role in a revival of a Richie Washington play. Actors were fans too, and Nick was a huge admirer of the unfortunately short-lived playwright.

"You realize this wouldn't even be an issue if you hadn't signed up for a role which required dancing. You know I love you, Nick, but…"

Nick sighed. "But I'm lucky I don't trip over my own feet. I know. Everybody knows." It was a joke at this point. He could do many things. He could put on a passable Australian accent, and had for "The Year It Rained." He could decorate a cake with bakery precision after "Sugar on Top." He was an admirable tenor. But absolutely, in no way, shape, or form, could he dance.

His brain and his feet had a feud which began at birth. They'd eventually hit a détente. His feet conceded on walking and running, but refused to cooperate beyond that. Nick had driven Russ Vukovich, Olympus's former fight coordinator, to tears when it came to sword fighting footwork.

Brian was one of the highest paid contract attorneys in the city. If anybody was capable of finding a way to save Nick's bruised ass, it would be him. Nick pulled out a stack of contracts and set them on Brian's wide redwood desk.

"There's got to be some way around this," Nick pleaded. "It was bad enough when she kept hinting it was time to meet my parents after a month. Then I had to deal with her at work and to top it off, she's a crappy teacher. I have no idea how she ever got her reputation for being the best instructor out there. I've had lessons for six weeks and I haven't learned a thing. I don't know a single step. I might even be dumber than when I started. We only have another month 'til the curtain rises. Colby and I are having fits." Nick would eventually recover from a single career disaster in a medium he didn't plan to return to. Colby, on the other hand, would likely never get another meeting with a potential backer if his first venture flopped as badly as they feared it would.

Nick wandered around Brian's office while the other man lifted the stack of papers on his desk. He looked over the Los Angeles cityscape and solemnly vowed to the Our Lady, The Queen of Angels, he would never, ever do another production with dance numbers if she got him out of his current situation.

Brian flipped in a few pages, and stopped at a section Nick had marked with a Post-It. "According to this, you are paying Sandrine for choreography and instruction. I see no reason why you can't be rid of her if you pay her fee."

"Thank you, God."

"You're welcome."

"Funny."

"Of course, this leaves you with another problem. The curtain lifts in a month. Who can you get to teach you that quickly? Essentially, you'll be starting from scratch," Brian said. "I can make some calls but you'll be paying through the nose at this late date. Does the production even have the budget for this?"

"I'll cover the cost if I have to. Thanks for the offer but don't worry about me. I have a line on somebody who is highly recommended." Okay, "highly recommended" was a stretch but he wasn't about to admit he needed more help on top of the contract extraction. Nick had already tried his next top seven choices and no matter how much money he threw at them, they remained unavailable for a short-term, last minute engagement. He was getting desperate and when he'd mentioned his situation to his Olympus co-star Chris Peck, he got an unexpected suggestion. Since he was desperate enough to consider it, Chris promised him a meeting which might lead to his salvation. He'd find out tomorrow but he was happier knowing he'd go into it with Brian's blessing.

"Nick?"

"Yes?"

"What are you going to do before you offer your new choreographer a contract?"

Nick knew the answer to this one. "I'm going to have you look at it before, during, and after it's signed."

"Good boy."

Now all Nick had to do was find a dance instructor to offer it to.

* * * *

Another dream ruined, squashed beneath her feet like a dropped Churro on the Santa Monica Pier. Ashleigh Jessup figured she should legally change her name to Goldilocks these days. She already had the blonde hair, and she'd seen every commercial building in a twenty-mile radius and found them to be either too big or too small. None of them were just right for her new location.

She had three months before she had to either renew her current lease or find a new and permanent home for Jessup Dance Studio. Ashleigh was still stunned her business had outlasted her lease. When she first opened her doors, she hadn't been sure she'd make it a year. To have been successful for five shocked everyone, her most of all.

She picked up the real estate listing she'd dropped and studied it again. The strip mall property in front of her had the identical floor plan as her current place. Ashleigh wanted much larger. Ideally, with one main studio area and one or two smaller private rooms which were rentable as private classrooms. This one wouldn't do.

"No go?" Caitlin Kelly yelled from the car.

"No go," she replied. Ashleigh climbed back into Stella, her trusty little Nissan, and started her on the second try. She was sure the car would last until Lease Day. If Ashleigh didn't move, she'd have the funds to buy a brand new one, making a major down payment and ending up with tiny monthly payments. If she moved her business, it would be the reverse. Either option was good so long as she got a new car out of the deal. Even Nissans didn't last much longer than fifteen years; Stella was half as old as she was.

"Too bad. It's a good location," Caitlin sympathized.

"It's not as good as the Duncan Building." Ashleigh sighed as she recalled her dream studio. She'd made an offer on the perfect space four months ago but had been outbid at the last minute. Since then, nothing she'd viewed had compared.

"It's gone. Move on." Caitlin took a draw on her iced green tea. Her friend had a personal interest in Ashleigh's potential new studio, being as she'd have first dibs on the private studio. Ashleigh had been Caitlin's personal instructor for going on ten years, back from when the two had met in college. Caitlin had branched off into music and acting as well as dance but she continued to work with Ashleigh regularly. "Where to now?"

"Home. Tomorrow is another full day of classes."

"Saturdays suck."

"Saturdays pay the bills," Ashleigh corrected. "Technically we could look at one more but honestly, I'm too wiped and it's half an hour from here. I say we blow it off and order in some Pad Thai, unless you're on a budget this week."

"No budget, but it'll have to be rice and veggies for me. I'm working next week."

Ashleigh jammed the gear shift back into Park. "Excuse me."

"I got the part!"

"You're supposed to tell me stuff like that."

"I got the call when you were checking out the building."

Ashleigh beamed at her friend. College had been a lot of fun, but after graduation, Ashleigh and her group of friends settled in for a long haul to achieve their dreams. It was great to see everybody's hard work finally paying off. "Call Sydney. Chris is working tonight. We'll celebrate."

Their mutual friend Sydney Richardson ran a charitable foundation which had gained public support since its inaugural gala back in February and was now doing well. Not to mention, she had a super-hot, super sweet boyfriend. Caitlin had another acting job, and they were beginning to come with near regularity. She also might have a super-hot boyfriend but she was being awfully cagey about it. Ashleigh's own business was booming. There wasn't much that could make things better for her. Except a super-hot boyfriend of her own.

It was a shame there weren't listings for that.

Chapter 2

Nick looked around the Jungle with undisguised interest. This was not a bar frequented by the Hollywood elite. This place might not have even heard of the word "elite." There were no private daises, no roped off VIP sections. Chris Peck, however, promised they offered a surprising number of microbreweries, so at least they had that going for them.

He took the bottle of Black Bear Pale Ale and waited for his friend's second surprise of the evening. Chris was in the middle of shooting a movie and had to be back at the set early the next day. He was making the introduction Nick had requested and heading straight home.

"Is your mystery recommendation really coming tonight or are you setting me up?" Nick asked. It was a perfectly reasonable question. He wouldn't put it past Chris to do something as low as dragging him here to watch him squirm first before taking him to the real meeting. Of course, it wasn't as low as the time he'd littered Chris's trailer with dozens of wrapped condoms the morning of his mother's visit, but exposing Nick to the Jungle was still pretty low. "How do you even know about this place?"

Chris pointed to a group of women standing near the stage. A couple of them looked familiar but he only recognized Chris's girlfriend, Sydney, by her red hair.

Nick was as shocked as anyone else when Olympus's most popular actor began dating the woman who won the show's fan appreciation contest the previous February. Chris had almost blown his chance with Sydney but he come back with a last minute save by recruiting several castmates to help with her charity fundraiser. Chris, Nick, and Sean all got involved in her beach volleyball tournament that introduced them to several of Sydney's friends, including one who was an actress and ended up with a recurring role at the end of the season.

At the moment, Nick was trying to identify the blonde Sydney was nudging as she waved at them. He thought he should know her but he couldn't place her.

"Syd's got a friend in the band. I've heard them before. They're pretty good," Chris said.

"Is your contact in the band?"

"Impatient, are we?"

"Little bit." Nick excused himself to pay the waitress for their drinks and when he turned around, the blonde was talking to Chris.

"Hey, Chris. Sydney asked me to come over and say hi. Hi."

Nick wished she were talking to him. She had her hair pulled up in a high ponytail and wore a pair of black satin capris she must have poured herself into. Paired with a red polka-dotted tied blouse and a matching headband, she looked like a Bond girl straight out of the sixties. He'd had the same reaction the first time he saw a similarly dressed pin-up girl poster in his grandfather's garage when he was fourteen. Her blue eyes and ruby lips drew his eyes against his will and it was all he could do to not throw wood right there in the middle of the club.

"Hi," he said, interrupting since Chris wasn't introducing him to the goddess himself. Bastard.

"Oh my god, you're Ares. I mean, you're Nick Thurston. It's nice to see you again."

See him again? Fuck. There was no polite way to say "Do I know you?" without coming off as a complete asshole. Nick smiled and offered his hand but his shock must have delayed his poker face.

"I'm Ashleigh Jessup. Sydney and I played against you and Sean Glenn at the Curse The Darkness Volleyball Tournament. We really appreciated it. You guys boosted our fundraising through the roof," Ashleigh continued, shaking his hand and politely giving him the out he so obviously needed.

"I remember. Glad to have helped." A vision of a sports tank and miles of tanned leg flooded his memory. Nick could definitely place her now. She looked completely different and just as hot.

When he focused on her again, Ashleigh was smirking. "I'll bet." She looked at him, and back at Chris. Her smile faded. "Oh, no. You didn't have Sydney rope me into one of your pranks, did you, Chris?"

"What? No. Ash, this is my friend, Nick. He has a real business proposition and he wants to talk to you about it. Do me a favor and hear him out."

"Okay," she agreed.

She waited, staring at him. Staring at him with those big, blue eyes of hers. Nick wanted to gaze into them all night. When she offered him a slow smile, he lost the battle and his dick snapped to attention. He'd never been more thankful for bad lighting in his entire life.

"Nick?" she prompted

What did she want? Oh, yeah, right. "I do need to talk to you. Can we set up a meeting? My theater company needs a choreographer and instructor."

Ashleigh pulled a business card out of her purse and handed it to him. "Give me a call tomorrow morning." She looked over her shoulder when the band took the stage. "Late tomorrow morning. We'll set up something for next week."

"For Monday. I'll call you tomorrow," Nick promised. Even if she was as inept as Sandrine at least the view during his lessons would improve. Besides, something about Ashleigh gave him a good vibe.

*

Holy crap, she'd just given her card to Nick Thurston. Ashleigh still got jittery talking to Chris on occasion, and she'd known the hit actor for months. Chris wasn't drop dead gorgeous, though. He had been but when he started seeing Sydney she had to shift him to the "not hot anymore" column. Nick, on the other hand was a free agent, and she was allowed to put him and his column anywhere she wanted.

She glanced at the man beside her. Shaggy brown hair with California blond highlights brushed the top of his shirt collar. Ashleigh watched Olympus; she knew Ares had a perfectly tanned six-pack hiding under his button-down. As coolly as possible, she leaned back a bit and glanced down. Cue the drooling—the ass and thighs in those slacks were definitely god-worthy. The best thing about togas was they offered equal opportunity objectification. Looking up, she saw long lashes framing his dark hazel eyes. Damn, she was hoping it was Hollywood magic. Why did the guys always get the lashes? It wasn't fair.

Sydney mentioned she thought he might have the personality to go with the looks, but she didn't know him that well yet. Mostly, she'd told Ashleigh tales of the practical jokes the actors played on each other.

So if a guy had the looks and the money and the personality, why did he need to talk to a small-time dance instructor? That's a good question, brain, Ashleigh complimented herself before she got distracted by the band taking the stage and the crowd bursting into whoops and applause. The opening guitar riffs rang out and Ashleigh decided she wouldn't worry about it until the morning. Her nights out were limited and she wasn't going to spend one worrying about work. She was out for a good time and this band was it.

Charlie Oscar Echo always brought the crowd to their feet. Ash and Sydney had been fans since college for one simple reason: to support Caitlin. At this point, the band didn't need their attendance to boost their numbers. Not when Caitlin was front-stage center with her bass guitar and every guy in the audience knew exactly who the black-haired beauty was. Ashleigh noticed Nick watching her friend with rapt attention. "Didn't you know she played?" she asked.

"Who is that?"

He didn't know? "That's Cait." No response. "You know, Caitlin Kelly?" Still nothing. The man was oblivious. "She played Psyche on your show last season for three episodes?"

The light dawned. Nick's jaw dropped and Ashleigh watched him try to form a sentence. "That's Caitlin? She's in the band?" Nick sounded stunned.

"Why do you think Chris let Sydney drag him here? We always come out to see her when the band is in town."

"She's good."

"She's very good," Sydney corrected as she appeared and grabbed Ashleigh's hand. "Come on, dance time."

It took about fifteen seconds for Ashleigh to get lost in the music. The band wasn't playing original stuff tonight but they had some killer covers. Good music, good company, good times. Ashleigh bounced a little when Sydney bumped into her. Not a hip bump; an "oops, wobbled on my heels because of tequila shots" bump. Sydney moved as well as anyone else on the dance floor but she tended to lose the beat after about a minute. Then she'd pause and start again. And lose it again. Ashleigh loved her little red-headed pal dearly but the girl could not dance.

Ashleigh was looking over her shoulder to see where Chris was, since he was going to be taking care of his date later and should be warned to switch her off the hard stuff now, when she saw it. She immediately downgraded Sydney's dancing skills from "dangerous" to "not all that bad" when she saw a man beside Chris apparently seizing on the dance floor.

No, no, no. Life was cruel. She recognized the tailored white shirt and navy pants. Ashleigh broke away from Sydney and squeezed through the crowd in her efforts to get back to Nick, who was clearly being tased. He wasn't dancing because his feet weren't moving. He was sort of swaying, not to the beat, and waving his arms a little. In all directions. With no rhythm whatsoever.

She knew the question before she asked it because she wasn't that lucky. "It's you, isn't it?" she shouted in Nick's ear.

He looked down at her in in surprise. He was surprised again when he realized he didn't look down by much since she was 5'11" in four-inch heels. "Me what?" he yelled back.

"You're the one who needs an instructor."

He gulped. She saw his tanned Adam's apple bob against his pale collar. "Is that going to be a problem?"

Ashleigh knew Nick's work. She mentally ran through all the shows and movies she had seen him in and came to a quick conclusion. Never, not once, had she seen him bust a move on screen. He did the "wrap his arms around her waist and talk to the girl on the dance floor" thing a couple times but Nick Thurston did not dance. She took a breath. It didn't matter. If she could teach four-year-olds when all they wanted to do was spin around in their tutus, she could teach a grown man.

"No problem."

She hoped.

Chapter 3

This was the place. The sign over the end unit proclaimed the spot to be "Jessup Dance Studio" and it was not at all what he expected. Ashleigh told him on the phone she had a small independent studio. But in a strip mall? How the mighty had fallen. Sandrine Gold had her own building with a huge classroom on the main floor and private studios on the second. Nick peered through the windows which ran along the upper half of the front wall. By the looks of it, Ashleigh's place had a small dance area, an office and a bathroom. Or maybe the bathroom was a dressing room. Either way, it didn't look promising.

It wasn't too late. He could call Brian and beg for a referral but he wanted to solve this problem on his own since he was the one who caused it. Nick tried the door again to see if it had magically become unlocked in the last three minutes.

Honestly, the location wasn't bad. It was just…average. It was a place suburban moms and dads would enroll their little darlings and deliver them in anonymous mini-vans. The kids would have lessons while their parents bought their generic groceries before picking the kids up and returning to their ordinary lives. Nick didn't need ordinary or average. He needed kick ass. Kick ass and fast and professional. So the question became, how much did he trust Chris?

The truth was he trusted him a lot. Chris knew what the role Otto Blackwood meant to him and his friend would never mess up a job. It was an unwritten rule between the pranksters. That meant Chris truly believed Ashleigh Jessup could help him out. Unfortunately, Nick didn't think his buddy truly understood how dire the situation was.

On the scale of "can't dance", there was not good, bad, very bad, a few more levels, and then Nick. He knew—hell, everybody knew—of his lack of skill when it came to footwork. Originally, he'd been thrilled when the theater signed Sandrine Gold as an instructor, and not only because they were dating. Her reputation was huge in the industry and everyone Nick spoke to swore she would be the one who straightened him out. Everybody lied.

He stuck the key in the ignition to turn on the radio but a shout from the opposite end of the parking lot made him yank it out immediately.

"Wait. Don't go. I'm here!" Ashleigh jogged up the sidewalk. Her blonde bangs stuck to her forehead and the sweat stains on her shirt displayed exactly how hard she'd run. The body hugging work-out wear verified all the curves her club outfit had promised on Saturday night. "I was hoping to make a better impression. I wasn't expecting you for another fifteen minutes," she said, breathing hard but not entirely out of breath. She pulled a key from a wrist band and invited him into the studio.

"You're a runner?" he commented. Man, between that and Saturday night's "hi", Ashleigh was going to mistake him for a genius.

"It helps me think and it gets me out of the studio. Do you? Run?"

"Regularly." His personal trainer whooped his ass if he didn't.

"Can you excuse me while I grab a quick shower or did you need to get started right away?" she asked.

"I'm early. I can wait."

"Great. Feel free to look around."

The building was old and tired but the studio was spotless. The walls were a forgettable beige but it was hard to see paint through all the posters Ashleigh had up. Ballet, jazz, hip-hop and what looked to be a well-framed square-dancing one hung in the corner of the main room. He stepped closer to check out the half dozen certificates and diplomas on the office walls, which ranged from Ashleigh's bachelor degree to her up-to-date certification in first aid.

Faster than he thought would be possible, Ashleigh reappeared, her long hair French-braided and tucked under itself. "Let's go into my office. How can I help you?" She pulled a bottled water out of the mini-fridge in the corner and offered him one. When he declined, she settled into the chair behind her desk and waited for him to speak.

Nick cleared his throat twice. "I'm playing Otto Blackwood at the Hawthorne Guild Theater in their upcoming Archie Washington revival of 'The Last Bachelor.' I'm also one of the producers. We need to hire a choreographer and instructor to work with us for the three musical numbers in the play. I mentioned that to Chris, who mentioned it to Sydney, who recommended you." He quoted the figure they were willing to pay and had to fight a laugh at Ashleigh's silent reaction. He hoped she didn't play poker since her face left absolutely nothing to doubt.

"It sounds like a great opportunity. When does the play open?"

"A month."

"I'm sorry. Did you say a month? And you haven't hired anyone yet?"

"We did have somebody but it didn't work out. Now we need a last minute replacement."

"Very last minute. What kind of rehearsal schedule are you looking at?"

"Whatever you can give us," Nick said. This meeting was going slightly better than planned. He would have been really worried if she'd agreed without these types of questions.

"I can do mornings, although I do have eleven o'clock classes twice a week. But I don't know if that would be enough time for you," Ashleigh offered.

Mornings worked. It would make for some very long days but he was used to it. "You'll mostly be working with me. I have footwork issues." Wow, that was a very mild, diplomatic description of his problem. "The rest of the cast did better in their lessons than I did."

"How big is the cast?"

Nick listed them off and was surprised when Ashleigh grinned at the final name. "I didn't realize this was Poppy's play. Okay, these dances won't be a problem," she said with confidence.

Technically it was his play but Nick wasn't going to correct her before she agreed to teach him. "You're a fan of hers?" His leading lady, Poppy Travis, was an actress who had spent most of the last five years on stage in New York City. Her wide-eyed portrayal of Darla Summers, the ingénue to his gigolo, was spot on. Colby Sinclair had been thrilled with their instant chemistry.

"I am but I was a friend first. Poppy and I go way back."

This was encouraging. Nick was getting a good feeling about this whole thing. "So are you interested?"

"Very, but I have a few more questions. Who did you originally hire who didn't work out?" she asked.

"I don't think that's important. Their contract has been terminated so we are free to hire whatever replacement we want." If he told her, she could figure out how far down the list of people he'd approached she was, and he didn't want to insult her. Not when she was so close to saying yes.

Ashleigh sucked back more water. Then she leaned back and waited.

"Sandrine Gold," he said. Fuck, Ashleigh was like some kind of master inquisitor. Mistress inquisitor? Oh, that wasn't a good line of thought. Ashleigh in tight leather with a crop. Maybe with some kind of mask. Yes, please.

"Of course it would be Sandrine Gold. What happened?"

"We experienced some personality conflicts and decided she wasn't a good fit for the production."

"I'm familiar with personality conflicts with Sandrine. In the name of full disclosure, you should know I worked with Sandrine, worked for Sandrine, a few years ago. I disagreed with her philosophies and eventually quit and opened up this place. It got ugly for a while but we mostly leave each other alone now." She put the cap back on the bottle and gave it a vicious twist, saying more about her pissed-off state than her words did. "You should know it may be an issue if she finds out I'm her replacement."

"Like I said, she's paid and gone. I think you're a good choice."

"And you're desperate."

Nick bit his cheek. "I wouldn't say desperate. Highly motivated to get started, definitely."

Ashleigh laughed. "Nick, I'll be straight with you. I'm a good teacher and you're offering a very nice salary. But realistically, you're talking about a severely truncated rehearsal schedule and this," she waved at the tiny office and small practice space, "is all I can offer you, unless you want to pay for a private studio. I also have classes to work around."

"I'll return the honesty and be straight with you. I can be flexible when it comes to the schedule, since it's mostly me you need to help. This location is fine unless we find it's more convenient to do it at the theater or at my place. I just need a good teacher. Besides, you are going to earn every single dollar I pay you because I have been told on countless occasions by numerous people that they'd have more luck teaching an elephant to dance than me."

She stared at him hard. "Okay, I'm in. If you're good with the morning schedule, we can start now. Let's see exactly how much help you need," she said. She strode out of her office into the middle of the floor. "Well, come on. Let's try a waltz." Ashleigh raised her arms. "Show me your frame."

*

"Wait. My what?" Nick asked.

Oh, crap. This was not a good sign. "Your frame." He didn't move. "How you hold your arms and body," she prompted.

Nick bowed his shoulders awkwardly and threw out his hands, almost smacking her in the face. For some reason he held his elbows in tight to his body. Ashleigh tugged on his forearms until he allowed her to adjust them. She took her own position, left hand on his shoulder and right hand in his. "Try to remember this as your closed position, okay?"

"My what?"

"Closed position. Both your arms are touching me, and both of mine are touching you. Like a closed circuit. Did Sandrine teach you turn steps or change steps?"

Please say yes.

"No. We didn't get very far. Do I need to know the technical terms? Can't you skip that part and teach me the moves?"

She could but it was going to make things more difficult. She and Sandrine always had different teaching techniques but for the other woman not to have even instilled the basics was unthinkable. Either that, or Nick wasn't exaggerating about being unteachable. "Let's give this a go," she said with more enthusiasm than hope.

Then she tested his footwork.

He hadn't exaggerated. Ashleigh was in so much trouble. Not in as much trouble as her feet but now she knew she needed steel-toed sneakers for Nick's next lesson to survive it. He wasn't bad. He was horrible.

One-two-three, one-two-three. There wasn't much to a basic waltz but she couldn't get that very simple idea into her partner's brain. She'd come across blocks before but never to Nick's extent. Not only did he show a lack of natural talent, he'd talked himself into believing he'd never be able to learn. From the sounds of it, the rest of the world had reinforced the idea. It was tragic. Moreover, it pissed her off. Everybody was capable of learning how to dance, and she was not going to give up. Ashleigh didn't want to ask what Sandrine had told him; she'd probably want to hunt the bitch and put her down, permanently.

Ashleigh shook it off. It wasn't Nick's fault. "Okay, now that I know where you're at, let's get started," she said, confidence clear in her voice. She was such a liar.

"Excellent!"

His enthusiasm lasted for the first thirty minutes.

"Just once, Nick," Ashleigh repeated for the umpteenth time. "One, two, three." She mirrored his steps and braced hard when he tried to do it again. She rocked a little on her feet but she stood firm.

"Why do you keep stopping me?" he asked. His body was as tight as his voice.

"Because we aren't dancing. We're doing this one step."

"We've been doing it for half an hour already."

"And we'll do it for another thirty. You student, me teacher. Again. Once. Left, right, left."

He did it correctly. Finally. "Good. Did you like the band on Saturday?" she asked. Ashleigh hadn't found a way through his block so she was trying to find a way around it. Distraction might be the key.

"What?" She felt his hand tense as he prepared to take another step but she stood still.

"Charlie Oscar Echo. What did you think of them?" She refused to move, knowing Nick had already talked himself into messing up the next three steps. Ashleigh kept eye contact with him, and wanted to flinch at the frustration which was simmering in them. He obviously wanted to do this correctly and knew he was screwing it up. She felt bad for the guy.

"They were pretty good for a cover band," he said.

"Chin up," she reminded him. Nick leaned into her in an attempt to force her to move. She pushed back. Damn, the boy had some fine forearms. His biceps were impressive, too. She'd be more impressed with him if he listened to her. "They're not really a cover band. They only play them in the Jungle. Mostly they do their own stuff. They're good."

Nick relaxed a fraction when he realized she wasn't going to give in. "Do you think you might be a bit biased?" he teased as he held their position.

"I'm a lot biased. Doesn't mean they aren't good,"

she replied, smiling. "Caitlin says they're going to record an album this summer."

"Do they have a label contract?"

Ashleigh squeezed his hand and pulled slightly, leading him into the next three steps and froze again. "Good. Not that I know of. It sounds like they've had some nibbles though. I think they're going to try the indie thing. Chin up. I wish you could have heard Caitlin sing lead vocals. She's mostly stuck doing back-up but the girl has pipes."

"You are totally biased."

"I already agreed with you. One, two, three."

It went like that for the next half hour. Twenty seconds of talking, one second of dancing. But they were good seconds. The distraction technique worked. If she kept Nick out of his own head, he got it right. She'd actually slipped in a double when she found out he was a Clippers fan and started to give him grief over it. He'd been so pissed at her he hadn't realized what he'd done.

His form was already improving, which was impressive. Her current working theory was Nick was capable of handling one instruction at a time. As long as he concentrated on his frame or posture, he didn't have mental space to worry about his feet. It wasn't a long term teaching strategy but for now she'd take it.

"That's a wrap," Ashleigh told him. "Good job."

"Interesting technique, not dancing," he said.

"Interesting student," she retorted. "Now that I've gotten a feel for you, I'll work something out for tomorrow."

"About tomorrow…"

Ashleigh waited. Nick seemed to be the type of person who spoke on his own terms. She waited him out. Besides, he wasn't hard to look at. His bronzed skin was slightly flushed, more from emotion than effort, and it brought out his blond highlights and the cut of his cheekbones. The extra color looked good on him. Okay, she couldn't imagine anything not looking good on him.

"Can we start before eight? I think we did okay today but I'm very concerned you won't get me to where I need to be in time for opening night."

"We did great, Nick, but yes, we can. Seven o'clock?"

"Seven works. Meet you here," he agreed.

That was incentive for an obscenely early morning.

Chapter 4

Next time Nick was setting his clothes out the night before. He'd almost been late as he debated which shirt he wanted to wear. The brown one complimented his eyes but the blue one had a better cut. Yeah, it was going to get all sweaty but he wanted to impress Ashleigh.

The day before, his confusion at Ashleigh's teaching technique had given way to anger by the time he arrived home. What a waste of a morning that had been. He stayed pissed off for another hour until he walked into his state-of-the-art kitchen with its almost-never-used stainless steel appliances and did a one-two-three step when he moved from the sink to the black marble island. The island was half of the reason he'd stopped. The other half was he'd shocked himself by doing the move correctly. So he'd paused a step away from his sofa and did it a second time.

One-two-three. Hot damn, it worked.

He backed up and did it again. And again. It worked until he tried to do two in a row and tripped over his own feet. That was a good place to stop. Nick figured if Ashleigh taught him that much in two hours he wasn't going to question her methods anymore. He semi-waltzed around his apartment for the rest of the afternoon and the following morning until he realized he was going to be late for their session. He didn't want to risk ticking her off. Nick was most definitely hot for teacher.

He made good time but his phone rang as he pulled into Ashleigh's parking lot. He didn't bother to look at the call display. "I'm here."

"I wish you were," the woman at the other end of the call said.

"Sandrine?" He didn't have time for this. "You wished I was where? Didn't you get your check?"

"I wish you were here. In bed. With me."

"Sandrine, that's not going to happen." Nick usually dated actresses for a reason; he knew how to manage their expectations about what he could do for their careers. When he started dating Sandrine, she hadn't expected anything from him. Until she found out the theater needed a choreographer and instructor. She had the qualifications and the reputation they needed so Nick would have hired her anyway. She'd been very grateful. Her gratefulness lasted a week before she started hinting for more. Her hints and his lack of process on the dance floor were the one-two punch that ended the relationship. Nick thought he'd finally learned his lesson. No more mixing business and pleasure.

"Nick, I know I screwed up. It won't happen again. I made it too one-sided. We can help each other."

"There isn't going to be an 'again.' We were both clear on what we wanted and it wasn't the same thing. I think we made the right choice when we went our separate ways." He didn't remind her she was the one who broke things off, calling him a selfish prick who wouldn't help his girlfriend and was bad in bed.

He resented that. He got her a job. And he definitely wasn't bad in bed.

"Nick, even if we aren't lovers, we can work together. Colby told me you were buying out my contract. You need an instructor. Desperately."

"I have one. In fact, I'm heading into a lesson as we speak, so I have to go."

"Wait!" He knew that tone. It was the one that preceded a screaming match. "Who is it?"

"Good-bye, Sandrine."

"Nick, I'm the best instructor in the city. In the state. You need me, you rat—"

End Call was a great button. He should have used it earlier before she soured his espresso buzz. He'd been in the zone. He was ready to waltz. In the two minutes he talked with Sandrine, she managed to suck out all the self-confidence Ashleigh had given him the day before. She was right. He desperately needed help. Ashleigh taught him three steps. He needed more. He was screwed and not the way he and Sandrine used to be.

* * * *

Nick Thurston was an exceptional actor. He was completely convincing as a self-confident student. He smiled. He joked. He paid attention. There was one thing he couldn't fake: his body tension. His hips didn't lie. Neither did the stiffness in his shoulders. He was even worse than he'd been the day before, and that was saying something.

"Nick, what happened? You were doing so well."

"Was I?"

"Yes. I'm a professional dance teacher. I'd know."

"Sandrine said I was unteachable."

Why was he talking about Sandrine? Wait. Ashleigh recognized this tactic. "Then you fired her ass as you rightly should have. You are teachable, Nick. Let me guess. Sandrine called you to remind you how lost you'd be without her. She said you needed to hire her again and she's the only person on the face of the earth who can help you overcome your stupendous failings as a dancer."

Ashleigh would have laughed if Nick's face weren't so stricken. "She didn't say stupendous failings," he protested.

"Nick, it's not personal. Lying is part of her business plan. If a student leaves, she tries to convince them to come back by any means necessary. She calls older students to play on their insecurities, like she did with you. She calls the parents of younger students and guilts them into classes they can't afford, claiming they are denying their talented child a chance at a successful future. If that doesn't work, she'll try something else. Sandrine will do whatever she needs to do to bring you back to the fold."

"And you won't lie to me?"

"I don't have to. I didn't promise to turn you into Fred Astaire. I promised to have you waltzing in three weeks as required for 'The Last Bachelor.' I can do that without threats."

"What about mental manipulation?"

This time she did laugh. "Oh, no, I'm going to manipulate the hell out of you, starting now."

The man was too cute. She wasted the first hour getting him back to zero. She spent the next hour getting him to waltz one combination at a time. By the time they entered the third hour, they hit their stride. At the end of hour four, Nick was up to four in a row before he lost it. Eventually he was going to have to be the person leading the waltz but they'd made tremendous advances in their first two days. "You are officially four times better than you were yesterday. That's in twenty-four hours, Nick. When Sandrine calls back, be sure to tell her so."

"I was doing it." He puffed his chest out in pride. "I've never done so well before."

"I know you were doing it. I was there," she teased.

"You're a good teacher."

"I'm modest, too. You are going to be ready with time to spare," Ashleigh promised. "You worked hard. Stretch out a bit and grab a water before you go."

He was still stretching when the studio's front door

burst open. "Hi, Miss Ashleigh!" Tonya, one of her precocious four-year-old students bounded into the room, braids bouncing all over the place. "Look, I have a new tutu. It's purple!"

The little girl's skirt was very purple and bedazzled with sequins. "It's very pretty, Tonya. You're early. Where's your mom?"

"She's in the parking lot. She's slow. We had to go next door to the Starbucks 'cause Andy had to go potty. Can I practice on the bar?"

"You go ahead, sweetie. No swinging," Ashleigh reminded the little girl.

"Who is that?" he asked.

"She's in my kiddy class. I don't know if you are up for a personal appearance but if you aren't, I can let you out the back door."

While Nick considered his options, Ashleigh crouched down and smiled at the little student who wandered over and decided to join their conversation. "Can I help you, Tonya?"

"Who is he?" the girl asked, pointing at Nick.

"He's a friend."

"Are you learning how to dance, too? I can show you how to twirl," Tonya offered.

"I'm fine, thank you."

The little girl pulled on one of her short black braids. "Are you sure? I'm a pretty famous twirler. I have forty-eleven likes on my YouTube video. Do you have any likes on your videos?"

Ashleigh nearly bit through her lip trying not to laugh as Nick's face ran through all the colors of the rainbow. She looked at his website and it had over a quarter of a million hits per month. His show had been nominated for a dozen various awards last season, eight the season before. Ashleigh wasn't going to spoil her fun and tell Tonya that. "He doesn't have any twirling videos at all, Tonya."

"You should make one right away. They're super popular!" the four-year-old advised.

She was definitely going to lose it. "Can you wait at the bar for a minute, sweetie?"

"Okay, Miss Ashleigh."

As the girl skipped off, Ashleigh tried to wipe the smirk off her face. "Seriously, her mom will be here any second. If you don't want to be seen, you should go now." She herded him toward the door. "I'll see you tomorrow. Seven o'clock."

He was in his black Escalade with the tinted windows closed when Tonya's mom finished lumbering up the sidewalk, lugging a toddler and a diaper bag. "She's inside, Suze," Ashleigh said as she stood at the door, watching Nick make an anonymous getaway.

Chapter 5

Ashleigh was capital "E" Evil. And likely capital "S" Sadistic. Why else hadn't she warned him four hours of mostly standing still would hurt worse than his first Cross-fit class? Of course, he'd felt good enough the night before to head out for dinner and hit a club. The pain hadn't settled in at that point. Nick groaned again. It was a good one; he sounded quite pathetic with the whine at the end. Hot water would probably solve most of his problems but the multi-head shower stall was all the way on the other side of his bedroom in his private bathroom, so very far from his nice soft California king-sized bed and bamboo sheets. He wanted his mother. Or his masseuse. Or painkillers.

Even his arms were sore. He noticed when he smacked the snooze button on his alarm clock for the fifth time. He should have turned it off but it hurt too much to roll to his side to find the switch. The snooze bar worked fine.

After the third smack Nick knew it was now or never for getting out of bed. He limped to the bathroom and decided not to care about the water shortage for once and enjoy the hot spray. He heard his cell phone beeping in the bedroom but stuck his head back under the rainfall showerhead.

Moving and caffeinated, he was on his way out the door to Ashleigh's studio when he got down to the latest messages. "Fuck!" He had to stop looking at his phone in the mornings.

He hated canceling at the last but he didn't have a choice. There was no way he could make the lesson once he factored drive time to the theater and back. Nick pulled into the parking lot and found four cars already there.

Colby Sinclair, Sandrine Gold, Sandrine's attorney, Gavin McGill, and surprisingly, Brian Alexander all waited for him. Brian and Colby pulled out a chair on their side of the table in the conference room; lines had already been drawn.

"What's the emergency?" Nick asked.

"I want my job back."

"No." That sounded simple enough. He looked at Brian, who shook his head. Apparently not.

"I was unjustly terminated," Sandrine continued. "Mr. McGill agrees."

Shit. Ashleigh called it. This is why lawyers were invented. "Brian?" he prompted.

"Ms. Gold believes you fired her in order to offer her job to your new girlfriend, Miss Ashleigh Jessup. Ms. Gold is threatening to file suit for damages and unlawful dismissal."

"I don't have a girlfriend," Nick said.

"It doesn't matter what you call that bit...woman. Having a personal relationship with her is no reason to terminate my contract," Sandrine said.

"Colby, Brian, a word?" Nick rose from the table, not bothering to check if the men were behind him. Once they were all in the hallway, he pulled the door closed. "What the fuck?" he asked quietly.

"Don't panic," Brian started.

"Too late. What the fuck?" Nick repeated.

"It's nothing. She has nothing. You cancelled her contract with full pay. Even if she goes ahead and files suit, she won't get anywhere. Who the hell is Ashleigh Jessup, anyway?"

"Jessup Dance Studio."

Nick watched as Brian ran the name through his mental files of everybody worth knowing in the industry. "I don't recognize the name."

"Neither do I," Colby added. "Why her?"

Nick shrugged. "She was available. She's a friend of a friend of Chris Peck's and he trusts her." She's also hotter than hell. He didn't feel any need to voice his last reason.

"Are you dating?" Brian asked.

"What? No." That was the last thing he needed clouding the issue. "I didn't even know Ashleigh when we fired Sandrine. Oh, I'm lying. I met her once, back in February at the volleyball tournament the day of the show's fan appreciation contest." He waited for Brian to nod remembrance at the mention. "I'd forgotten about her until Chris reintroduced us this past Saturday night. We had our first lesson on Monday and our second one yesterday. I haven't seen her yet today. That is the extent of my contact. Literally, there's been nothing else."

Brian smiled broadly. "Fantastic. Do yourself a favor and continue not to date her. It will play better if something happens."

"I don't plan to date her. I'm no longer fishing in the industry pond. But didn't you just tell us nothing was going to happen?"

"It's a precaution," the lawyer hedged. "Would you like to be with us when we toss her out on her ass?"

"If I leave now, I may be able to make up some rehearsal time with Ashleigh." Nick looked at the director. "Let me know when you schedule a full rehearsal and I'll pass it along. You'll like her, Colby. I've almost got the waltz down already." He was exaggerating, partially to make Ashleigh look better, but he wasn't doing it by much.

"She must be some kind of miracle worker. She's really that good?"

"She really is. Do you need me to stay?"

"No, we've got this. Go rehearse. I'll call you later this morning after we deal with this."

There was one other item he needed to address. "Brian, I'd be very interested to know how Sandrine knew I'd been meeting with Ashleigh. Very interested."

The lawyer's eyes got bigger for a second before he smiled in agreement. "I'm very interested in that, too. I'll let you know."

"Great. Call me later, okay?" Nick wasn't looking forward to the bill for this out-of-office visit but it would be worth it if Brian made Sandrine go away permanently. Now all Nick had to do was explain to Ashleigh why he was late and that he might have brought Sandrine back into her life.

* * * *

This was going to be an expensive girls' morning out but, damn, she was going to come out of it looking good. Ashleigh grasped the skirt of the 1940s party dress and spun in front of the full-length mirror in the back of Vintage Review. The tight bodice moved with her and the skirt flared out like it was supposed to. The coral silk was slightly worn at the seams but that was to be expected on a vintage find like this one.

Applause floated over from the sofa at the end of the row of dressing rooms. Sydney Richardson, in a short-sleeved, thigh-high dress with a high Chinese-styled collar, let loose a wolf-whistle at her. "You are absolutely getting that dress," she said.

"I am," Ashleigh agreed. "With those silver sandals I got in April, oh, yeah." Doing her hair in an era-appropriate style would be a pain in the ass but she could definitely rock the look.

"Now all you need is someplace to wear it," the third woman in the dressing rooms added. Vanessa Vaughn, the assistant manager slash friend and volleyball teammate slash vintage clothing dealer, had been supplying Ashleigh's fashion fix for years. They'd met one day when Ashleigh had been making the rounds of her favorite second-hand shops and had dropped into Vintage Review on a whim. It was Vanessa's first day on the job and she'd set Ashleigh up with two divine outfits. They'd been friends ever since.

"Vanessa, how many times have I told you if you find me a dress like this, I'll find somewhere to wear it." Ashleigh twisted her hips, enjoying the sounds the material made as it swayed around her. She would find the perfect place. Not some place to be admired. Some place she could dance. Such a masterpiece deserved to be properly displayed.

"Bingo!" Sydney exclaimed under her breath. Ashleigh got a bad feeling in the pit of her stomach when Vanessa, who was looking at Sydney's phone over her shoulder, stuck her fingers into her three-inch afro and bit her lip.

"Syd, can you do that?" Vanessa asked.

"Well, I can't but Chris can. He's coming up to a break in his shooting schedule and has a couple days off from filming. He said he wanted to take me out someplace nice for my birthday on Saturday and I mentioned a night out with friends. I think it'll be nice, don't you?"

"I guess some people would call Domino 'nice.' You know, if they ever got in," Vanessa said, her voice heavy with sarcasm.

"You asked for a night out and he picked Domino?

Nice. You'll rock it in that dress," Ashleigh agreed.

"We. We are going to Domino. Me and Chris, you and Nick, and Vanessa and her hottie of the week."

Now this impromptu shopping trip made sense. "Syd, sweetie, I'm not seeing Nick."

"On what planet do I have a boyfriend? But I'll bitch later. You said Nick. Chris and Nick. If we're talking about your Chris, Sydney, that would mean Ash's Nick is Nick My-Panties-Just-Combusted Thurston? Damn, Ash, why didn't you say something?" Vanessa shouted.

"Because we're not dating. I have no idea why Syd thinks we are." She wouldn't mind, if she weren't working for him. But she was and that was that. At least dancing with him provided lots of fantasy fodder.

Sydney smiled. "They met last weekend at the Jungle. Charlie Oscar Echo was playing. He looked interested."

"He wasn't interested."

Vanessa dropped beside Sydney on the couch and nudged her. "Tell me more, tell me more."

"We—me and Syd and Chris—were at the Jungle on Saturday to watch Caitlin. Great freaking show, by the way. Sorry you missed it. Nick was there. Believe me, there was no interest," Ashleigh insisted. It was half a lie. There didn't seem to be any obvious interest coming her way. Sure, she'd caught Nick staring at her while she was on the club dance floor but he hadn't made a single move on her during their classes.

She wasn't sure why he'd canceled this morning's session at the last minute but he promised to show up before her afternoon classes to explain and reschedule. In the meantime, since she suddenly had the morning free, she'd called up Sydney and turned it into a treasure hunt.

The shop door chimed and Vanessa peeked around

the corner. "Hi, Rita. Come over to the cash. I have the outfit I told you about set aside," she called to the new arrival. "I'll be right back. I want more gossip," she said to Sydney before dashing off.

"What are you doing?" Ashleigh shouted at Sydney.

"Getting you a date?" the redhead answered.

"Syd, he hasn't shown the slightest sign he likes me. Also, movie star."

"Yeah, because that last reason worked so well for me." Sydney had a point. Chris had been offered up as the grand prize in Olympus's fan appreciation contest. It was an inspired marketing idea, having the king of the gods acting as somebody's slave for a day. Ashleigh had entered it herself, to no avail. Unfortunately the contest winner was never notified and Sydney had no idea she'd won until Chris showed up on her doorstep one Saturday morning. The pair got off to a rocky start but it eventually worked out for everyone involved. Nobody expected Chris to stick around after the contest ended but the two had been inseparable ever since.

"Syd, it's not happening."

"If you say so. Do I call Chris for Saturday?"

"For yourself? Sure. You guys should definitely go to Domino. You'd be crazy not to. Make them all drool, especially Chris. But make the reservations for the two of you."

"Okay, I won't ask Chris to invite Nick. But you're coming to my birthday supper."

Ashleigh stood and twirled in her new dress. "I can live with that. I'll wear my dancing shoes."

Chapter 6

Nick sat in his Escalade, staring at the strip mall across the street. He hadn't noticed on Monday or Tuesday, but Ashleigh drew the blinds in the windows once she started a class. It made sense since the building faced south and would heat up quickly with the sun beating into the closed exercise room. If Sandrine had been watching him, the closed blinds would have prevented her from seeing anything beyond him entering the studio. There was nothing to misinterpret as a "girlfriend" vibe. He couldn't shake the bad feeling he'd picked up at the meeting. If she was watching, he'd rather move lessons to the theater sooner rather than later to deny Sandrine future ammunition. Nick didn't doubt Sandrine would take any opportunity to mess with him or Ashleigh.

In fact, his ex was another layer to all the reasons why he shouldn't date his new instructor. It had killed him not to give Ashleigh even the slightest innuendo. His cock ached for the entire ride home after his classes. She smelled incredible, and he wanted to groan whenever she put her soft, strong hands on him. She was either running a fever or she was the hottest woman he'd ever held. But he couldn't risk making a move. He wanted professionalism and that's what she gave him.

It was too bad. He'd love to innuendo the hell out of Ashleigh. He liked being with her. Nick got mad all over again when he realized he needed to tell her it might be unsafe for her to be seen with him.

He waited until Ashleigh flipped the sign in her window to closed, with the little clock indicating she'd be back at two. He pulled a quick U-turn and zipped into her parking lot as she was getting into her car.

"Hey, can we talk?"

"Nick? Is your meeting done?"

"Can I buy you lunch?"

"I've got to run an errand and be back in an hour."

Nick popped the locks on the passenger door. "I'll drive you." When she hesitated, he added, "Sandrine Gold and her lawyer paid me a visit this morning."

Ashleigh was seated and buckled up before he got the car back into Drive.

"So what did the woman I'm specifically not calling a spawn of Satan want with you?"

"First she made accusations against me. Then against you. Then against me again. Then Brian kicked her ass and her lawyer's ass. It was beautiful."

Ashleigh opened and closed her mouth a few times. "I have no idea where to start."

*

What the ever-loving fuck? Nick was by no means the first man to scramble her brains but he definitely did the best job of it. Fifteen seconds of talking led her to fifteen different questions. Ashleigh chewed on her lip as she sorted herself out.

In no order of importance: Hot damn, Escalades were a nice ride. The thick cushy seats alone were divine, let alone the buttery soft leather covering them. She didn't feel a single bump along the road, even when they hit the patch of construction at the freeway onramp. Sandrine Gold had no business threatening her. Nick, maybe, but not her. Finally, to hopefully put the rest of it in context, she asked, "Who is Brian?"

"Brian is Brian Alexander, my lawyer. Great guy. Very smart."

"Why was he at a meeting you had with Sandrine?"

"Somehow Sandrine saw us together and accused me of firing her so I could offer you, my replacement girlfriend, her old job." He held up a hand. "I know. It's bullshit. I still have to deal with it. In the meantime, your contract is intact. I do think, for security's sake, we should move rehearsals to the theater. Starting tomorrow."

"We can do that. A seven o'clock start?"

"Yes. We'll make it work. Can I ask you something?"

"I don't promise to answer, but you can ask."

"What did you mean when you said you had some problems with her?" Nick asked.

Ashleigh didn't want to get back into that sticky situation but she didn't have a lot of choice. "When I worked for her, I signed a contract stating when I left I wasn't allowed to contact any of my former students for two years. It's a standard non-compete clause. I didn't contact them but that didn't mean they couldn't contact me. A lot of them did. It pissed her off. The clause expired and for the last three years, I've been legally allowed to poach her clients at will."

"Did you?"

"Hell, yes. I'm not a saint. Besides, it wasn't like she didn't go after mine." For the first two years, it had been a constant battle to keep a client base since the non-compete clause ran one way. Sandrine approached every client Ashleigh took on in an effort to drive her out of business. The dance legend even offered free lessons for new students who transferred over from Ashleigh's studio. Fortunately Sandrine's greed never stayed repressed for long. As soon as the free lessons ended, Ashleigh's students came back. She charged them a premium rate since they technically weren't returning students. Like she said, she wasn't a saint. "That's when we mutually agreed to an unofficial cease-fire."

"I think the cease-fire may be over." Nick followed Ashleigh's pointing finger as he pulled into the street she indicated. "Where are we going?"

"Right at the next set of lights."

"Where specifically are we going?"

Ashleigh pulled the listing from the weekend out of her purse. "A potential new studio location." She gave him the address and he repeated it into his GPS. Soon a female British voice told him to take the next right. With the directions out of the way, Ashleigh returned to her questions.

"Does Brian think we're going to have any problems with my contract? I don't want to get into another legal battle with her."

"Brian says no but I don't trust Sandrine. That's the primary reason behind moving my lessons. Plus, you need to start working with the rest of the cast so we might as well start now."

"I can do that." Ashleigh pointed to a three-story storefront with apartments on the upper levels. "There."

Nick pulled into an empty space at the curb. "Damn, it's too bad you weren't here now."

"Why?"

"We're about half an hour from my place. It's much closer than your current studio."

Ashleigh cupped her hands on the dirty front window and squinted into the dark interior. "Hey. This isn't bad." Nick joined her at the window and she pointed out the features she saw from the listing. Huge open floor plan, hardwood floors, old but serviceable. Three small rooms off the main area, allowing for two private studios and an office if she was lucky. She needed a key to examine the rest.

"It's a lot larger than your current place," Nick said.

"I need the space. It's time to go big or go home."

"Are you going to make an appointment to see the inside?"

Ashleigh looked at the listing again. It was at the very top of her budget. Her imaginary budget with her highly optimistic projections. On the other hand, she'd have apartment rental income, too. It was the second nicest place she'd seen. It might even be tied with the Duncan Building, which was her unit of measure. "I think so."

"It looks good. Good location," Nick commented.

She looked around and pictured the area in her head. He was right. She was on the edge of her self-imposed border. Any further away from her current location and she'd lose too many of her current students. But, as Nick noted, it put her within spitting distance of a load of much wealthier ones. She had to do some number-crunching. If she wanted this place, which she was ninety percent sure she did, she was going to have to work for it.

"Okay, I'm done here. As for work, we'll start at the theater tomorrow morning if that works for you." She'd been planning what she needed to do with the full cast since Monday and couldn't wait to get started. This opportunity was going to pay off in more than an unexpected influx of cash in her slow season. Jessup Dance Studio was going to get some major publicity out of it. She owed Sydney huge.

"Excellent. Let's get you back to work."

Chapter 7

Nick knew Ashleigh was smart. A person didn't run a successful business for five years without brains. He asked her about her requirements for a new location and they got into a ten minute debate about real estate financing on the drive back to her studio. That's when he asked, "You majored in Dance, right?"

"Yes, at UCLA."

"What was your minor?"

"Double major. The other one was Business."

"Figures." She was seriously smart. It was sexy. It was even sexier when she assumed he could keep up with the conversation. Not once since Ashleigh had met him had she assumed he was just a pretty face. Nick couldn't do the regular college thing but he'd managed to complete a political science degree through some online and very carefully-chosen classroom courses.

Nick pulled into her parking lot and let his SUV idle in the parking stall in front of her front door. Ashleigh had her head down, checking her phone calendar for a block of time to reschedule his missed lesson. He didn't have a day to waste.

"A-ha!" she crowed in victory before she looked up, smiling. Then the smile disappeared off her face and she plastered herself against her seat.

"What's wrong? What happened to the 'a-ha'?" he asked.

"Remember when you said Sandrine might do something stupid? Check out the silver Mazda across the road."

Nick chanced a glance over his shoulder where Ashleigh had been looking and winced.

"Why does he have a camera? It's not like she doesn't know you hired me," Ashleigh asked.

Nick braced for a slap. "You know how I mentioned she claimed I fired her because I was sleeping with you? To prove the accusation, she's going to need proof we're in a relationship."

"But we're not."

"I know and I'll bet Sandrine knows. But at this point I don't think she cares about the truth."

"So what are we going to do?"

He had no idea but he did have a cell phone. "Brian, I think we have a Sandrine situation going on here."

Nick explained what was going on. His lawyer was not amused. "Can you sit tight for five minutes? Don't move a muscle."

"We can do that."

"I'll call you right back."

Nick looked at Ashleigh, who looked at her watch. "I can give you ten minutes before I have to get inside."

Brian took six. "Okay, you're good. Just go about your business normally. Keep watching your backs 'til I get this sorted."

This was a complication Nick did not need. Photos in the hands of someone as unpredictable as Sandrine was a disaster in waiting. Fortunately, he was in good company.

Ashleigh leaned forward to look again, and the air-conditioning caught her hair, blowing a hint of her citrusy perfume his way. God help him, she smelled good. She needed to do something to fuck up in a hurry because she was much too attractive at the moment.

"Do you think he has such a huge, telescoping camera lens to compensate for a tiny penis?" she asked.

Jesus, it might even be love. Nick burst into laughter. As much as he didn't want to end their not-date, he gestured to the dashboard clock. "You'd better go if you don't want to be late."

"Okay, see you tomorrow morning."

Her hand was on the handle and she was halfway out the door before he blinked. "Wait!"

Nick snatched the listing which had fallen between her seat and the console. He strained against the seatbelt to hand it to her and she leaned back in to grab it. Her knee slipped on the seat and suddenly his mouth was an inch from her lips. Her lip-gloss tinted, plump, smiling lips. She exhaled in surprise and he smelled the grapefruit gum she'd offered him earlier. She was delicious in all forms. All he had to do was lean forward and kiss her and she'd know he wasn't worried about her professionalism anymore.

"Thanks."

Then she was gone.

*

What was she thinking? She almost kissed Nick after he told her about his trouble with Sandrine and after Brian told them to stay out of trouble. Nick was definitely trouble. It was all she could do to keep from jumping him, especially the way he said "wait" and licked his lower lip. He had to know how abso-fucking-hot he looked when he did that. Although, if he did, it meant he did it on purpose, which meant he thought of her in unprofessional ways. It was too bad she couldn't return the favor.

But Nick was gone now and she had to get to work. Ashleigh made sure the blinds were completely secure before she greeted the two women waiting in her office. "I'm pissed off so be prepared to work."

"We love you too, Miss Ashleigh," Caitlin sing-songed back.

Ashleigh threw herself into the choreography in an effort to get her mind off the untouchable Nick Thurston. It worked for a while. Caitlin and her partner worked for an hour on the choreography for Charlie Oscar Echo's new video. When she ended the session, the second woman bolted but Caitlin made herself at home in Ashleigh's office. After helping herself to a diet Coke from Ashleigh's fridge, Caitlin turned to her friend and asked, "Did you work it out yet?"

"Work what out?" Ashleigh asked.

"The bug. Out of your ass. Because whatever it is, I suggest you remove it before Sydney's big party on Friday night."

"Sydney's having a big party? When did this happen? Last I heard it was a fancy supper with Chris taking her to Domino afterward."

"You're way behind. I'll catch you up after you catch me up. What has you in such a tizzy?" Caitlin asked.

Caitlin had stuck by her for her first go-around with Sandrine. In fact, Caitlin had always remained a private client, refusing to sign with the school even when Ashleigh was teaching there. When Ashleigh was fired, Caitlin was her number one source for student referrals. She was the perfect person who would understand where Ashleigh was coming from. "I was informed through reliable third parties that Sandrine Gold is back on the warpath again."

"Do you keep a bottle in your office? I think we're going to need some hard stuff if that witch is involved."

"Actually, I do." Ashleigh pulled a mickey of vodka out of her desk drawer. "Grab me a soda." She topped up their pop cans and filled Caitlin in on the entire story.

"Are you joking?"

"My sense of humor isn't that good."

Caitlin held out her can again in response. "This calls for a double."

Ashleigh happily obliged. "I've got kiddy class in an hour so I'll stick with what I have. She raised her bottle. "To Sandrine Gold getting screwed in the least fun way possible."

"At least she'd be getting some at all," Caitlin muttered.

"You too? Who?"

"Nobody. That's the fucking point. The not-fucking point. Whatever. At least it sounds like you and Nick have possibilities."

"I don't. Nick told me outright having a relationship with Sandrine is part of the reason he couldn't work with her. If I want to keep him as a client, I have to play it absolutely straight, which means no flirting at all. It's killing me. You didn't tell me he was so flirt-worthy when you worked with him." Her vodka and 7-up was going down much too easily. Damn Nick and his fabulous abs and knee-melting smile and uber-sexy brain. She was in deep trouble. "You should have warned me."

"I'm pretty sure I drooled when I was sitting on your sofa talking about the toga fittings," Caitlin countered.

"I remember but it doesn't matter because I don't get to go there. How about you? It sounds like you aren't getting any either, hotshot. What's up with that? I thought you had somebody on the line."

Caitlin shrugged. "I thought I might but it turns out I don't and he isn't. Besides, I don't have time to date. I have parts coming out of my ears." Her face burst into a blinding smile.

"Oh my God, tell me!"

"I'm allowed to say now. I've got a job next week.

It's Chris's movie. I'm in four scenes."

"That's awesome." For Caitlin. It sucked for her. Now she'd be invited to parties where she'd have even more chances to drool pathetically after Nick, who would undoubtedly be there to support his friend. Shake it off, Ash. This is a good thing, she thought.

"I need to take some R and R as well," Caitlin hinted.

The smile in her voice gave her away. Ashleigh bit on the extended hook. "Why?"

"In Ash-speak, it's not officially official yet so I'm not saying I have to rest up for my new regular series role on a drama that rhymes with 'Sho-lympus.'"

That's when Ashleigh lost her mind for her friend, and all thoughts of Nick went right out the window.

Chapter 8

Nick slapped his phone to turn off the god-awful ringing. It didn't stop. What the hell? He pried his eyes open and focused on the clock on the nightstand. Maybe he'd set it wrong. He didn't have to get up for another hour, which gave him lots of time to get to the theater to meet Ashleigh for rehearsal. Mmm, Ashleigh. He'd been dreaming about her. They'd been back in school. He was the student and she was the strict teacher…

The ringing started again, not on his cell but on the house line. "What the hell?" He answered it. "Nick Thurston."

"Mr. Thurston, we have a Miss Ashleigh Jessup at the gate."

"Ashleigh? Send her up." What the hell? How did she even know where he lived? Nick didn't think she was the stalker type but he'd been wrong before. He didn't have time to shower but he took a minute to brush his teeth and run a comb through his hair before he meet her at his front door.

"Did you see?" she greeted him.

"Ashleigh, it's six in the morning. See what?"

"Is that any way to talk to your girlfriend?"

"Excuse me? Again, six in the morning. How did you get my address?" She threw her cell phone and it bounced off his chest and onto the floor. "Ashleigh!"

"Chris gave it to me. And shouldn't you be calling me 'babe' or 'sweetheart' or something?"

His brain finally kicked in. "Oh, fuck. Sandrine? Are there pictures?"

"Yes. Lots. Even a couple of us kissing."

Nick froze. Unless someone had invented technology

which recorded and printed his dreams, he was confused. "We haven't kissed."

"I know! The rest of the world, however, thinks we were going at it like bunnies in your Escalade. I thought you said he was a P.I. for Sandrine's lawyer, not a paparazzi."

"Paparazzo. Paparazzi is plural," he corrected automatically before he refocused. "Show me the pictures."

Ashleigh snatched her phone off the foyer floor and reset the screen. Her hand shook as she handed it to him. "There are four of them."

Nick scrolled through the shots. As he suspected, three of them were taken when Ashleigh leaned in to grab the listing he held out for her. From that angle, it did look like she leaned in for a kiss. The fourth picture was disturbing. It was of the two of them outside the building Ashleigh was considering. He was snugged up beside her and she was looking up at him smiling. Nick remembered that; it was seconds after they'd peered through the window. This was bad. It meant not only had the photographer followed them, he'd also sped back to the dance studio's current location to catch them on their return trip. The little shit was well informed. "Okay. Coffee first. Then we deal."

Ashleigh took Irish cream in her coffee. Even at six in the morning. Of course, she'd been up for almost two hours already. The more reputable gossip columns stuck with the facts about Ashleigh and speculated about their relationship. The worst of the worst tabloid sites offered quotes from "Nick's devastated ex" which badmouthed Ashleigh and accused her of hurting Nick and his career. Those stories ranged from Ashleigh claiming to be pregnant in order to force him to dump Sandrine, to making him quit Olympus.

"Did you read the last one yet?"

"I'm getting to it." Hollywood Secrets was a nearly legitimate news site. They had people everywhere in the industry and were accurate a scary high percentage of the time. This time, however, they screwed the pooch. "Oh, fuck me."

"I would, but it seems I already have."

Nick read the offending snippet a second time, just to make sure he got the full impact of the accusations. "Nick Thurston may have to give up the title role in his new play since he seems to be off the market permanently. 'The Last Bachelor' seems to be taken after he fired renowned choreographer and long-term girlfriend Sandrine Gold. Thurston's new squeeze Ashleigh apparently convinced him her moves on the dance floor were as good as her moves in the bedroom." He read it again. "Ashleigh, I am so sorry."

"Don't apologize. You didn't leak any of this shit."

"It makes it sound like…"

"I know what it makes it sound like, Nick. It sounds like I pulled a Sandrine manoeuver. The irony is hilarious." She did an excellent job of joking but when her voice broke on the last word, so did his heart. Her smile lasted a fraction of a second longer before it started to dissolve and she hid her face behind her hands. "I'll be alright. Give me a minute. I can do this."

There was nothing he could say to fix it so he didn't try. Instead he wrapped her in his arms and tried to block out the world. Ashleigh's shoulders hitched a couple of times but she didn't make a sound, which made it worse. Nick wasn't fond of dramatics but once he knew what the problem was, he was halfway to solving it. He didn't know which of the many insults in the piece she was responding to most.

When her head dropped to his chest and Ashleigh whispered a quiet "okay" he let her go. Not entirely. Nick kept his hands on her arms and ran his hands up and down her smooth skin. "What do you want to do?"

It took her a moment to reply but when she did the answer was pure Ashleigh. "I want to teach you how to waltz so well you'll be able to do it in your sleep."

"What about the rest of it?"

"I'm new at this but I'm pretty sure you can't do a thing about the rest of this, can you? They're allowed to insinuate I got this job on my back." She tried to smile again. "Forget laid. I didn't even get a kiss to seal our deal."

That part he could fix. Before his common sense had a chance to kick in, Nick slid his hand around the back of Ashleigh's neck, and pulled her forward to kiss her. A quick peck to seal the deal. He was supposed to stop after a second but he couldn't. He smelled a hint of coffee and whisky and felt a smile on her lips. She opened her mouth the slightest bit, and he refused to pull away for anything.

She leaned closer and he took advantage. Her mouth was soft and warm and he wanted to stay there for hours, tasting her. His hand in her hair held her fast so he could deepen the kiss. Ashleigh tilted her head back to allow it. The thing she did with her tongue encouraged him more.

He managed to ignore the beep of an incoming text, and the call from the gate. But when both went off at the same time, Nick had to end it. It nearly killed him. He tried to pull away but he went back to touch her lips one more time. "Fuck, Ashleigh. Fuck."

"I know."

*

Boy, did she know. It was a good thing a chair was

close by because her knees were jelly. Her brain and her body reeled from the kiss. It was much better than she'd imagined it would be.

She'd imagined a lot. Kissing a toothpaste-fresh Nick while he was suffering from bed head was way up on the list. The whole holding-her-still-while-he-kissed-her blew the top off the charts. "Oh, that was bad."

"Bad? Are you kidding?" Nick frowned, clearly offended at her rating.

"Yes. No. The kiss was awesome. Maybe my best ever. We can never do it again."

"If it had been worse, could we do it again?"

"If it had been worse, it wouldn't be an issue."

"I don't understand."

"I am your instructor. You are a paying student. Kissing you is completely unprofessional. Let's not forget dangerous. See item one: Sandrine."

"But it was a good kiss, right?" Nick pressed. "I thought it was good."

"Exceptional," she agreed. "Which is why I'm saying never again, Nick."

"I understand."

She was glad one of them did. Because it sucked out loud. It had been…She couldn't remember the last time she'd been on a date, let alone the last time she'd been kissed so thoroughly. Her body yelled in opposition at her "no more" declaration as evidenced by the heat blooming between her legs and her damp panties.

It wasn't that she didn't want to date. She liked being one of a couple, having a partner to come home to and share her day. It simply wasn't easy to find a guy to do it with, especially as a woman who owned her own business. At first her occupation was brag-worthy for her man of the moment—yep, Ashleigh owned a dance studio. When the reality of working six days and four nights a week sank in, she became a selfish, uptight workaholic who didn't care about anybody else instead of the smart, powerful, independent woman she'd been a week earlier. Eventually, it became easier to skip part one to avoid part two. Easier emotionally. Her body missed the fun moments of part one.

"I need to get properly dressed. Can you see to Chris? The gate let him through and he should be at the door any minute."

"No problem." Maybe she ought to stand over an air conditioning vent on the floor and let the breeze blow up her skirt to cure her full body flush.

Nick disappeared up the staircase, and she found a floor vent to wait over while Chris pulled up the driveway. "How are you doing? You sounded rough on the phone," he asked as soon as he entered the house.

"Nick let me cry on his shoulder and now I have booze." She lifted her coffee cup. "I think that's as good as I'm going to get for a while."

Chris hugged her. "Call Syd," he whispered in her ear. "She's had some practice with this. Caitlin, too. I'm sorry it's happening but you'll be okay."

He was such a sweetheart. No wonder Sydney was head over heels for the boy. She hugged him back and, while nice, it wasn't as good as being held by Nick, not even when they were dancing at arm's length. "Thanks."

"Since you're here, I need a favor," he said as he let her go.

"Hit me."

"It's about Sydney's birthday party on Friday."

"Caitlin said. What happened to dinner out with you and dancing at Domino?"

Chris frowned at her with a touch of helpless puppy

dog in his eyes. "I may have gone a little overboard with invitations to dinner. And by a little I mean a lot. It sort of turned into a full-blown party. Help me, Ashleigh Jessup. You're my only hope."

"What do you need? Precisely?" she asked.

"You can't have her as a dance instructor. She's mine." Nick reappeared, wrapped his arms around her waist and spun her away.

Damn, she was up against his chest again. His very defined, powerful chest. Why wasn't she teaching him how to Salsa? She could be all over him with some sexy shimmying if she was teaching him some Latino moves. Instead she had to stay away from him, thanks to a very staid European box step. But since she was here…

"I don't think that's what he's interested in." She very casually copped a feel when she patted his chest, and quickly stepped away so it wouldn't be too obvious. If she wasn't allowing herself to kiss him again, feeling him up was definitely out of bounds.

"I need contact numbers for a few of Sydney's friends so I can text them the details. Can I send you a list?" Chris asked.

"Sure. If you want, you can send me the details and I'll organize them on my end."

"I'd appreciate it." Chris sighed. "Especially since that's the reason I really came over. Giving you two a hard time was an extra."

"What do you mean, why you came over?"

Chris waved his cell phone. "I got hacked. Thank God I moved everything personal off here when Sydney and I started dating. Miserable hackers, may they all burn in hell with syphilis. Not only did they get in, they changed some stuff, including my contacts. I don't have your actual number anymore."

"That sucks, Chris," Nick sympathized.

"Also, change your passwords. All of them. Daily for the next week or so," Chris advised. "I heard they hit a few others."

"Will do. Ash, do you mind if I talk to Chris for a second? There's a great view from the pool deck." He pointed through the kitchen door, through the decadently decorated living room to the wall of glass windows which looked over the city to the ocean in the distance.

"No problem." She knew she had an awed grin on her face and didn't mind the looks from the guys as she appreciated the view. She trailed her hand along the buttery soft black leather sofa as she wandered to the patio doors. She almost walked into the glass when the full-length lap pool came into view. Shit, he'd better finish up with Chris quickly. If she got to stay here too long she was never leaving.

Chapter 9

Nick was tired and in pain and he didn't have anybody to blame but himself. He kind of liked it. Ashleigh ran him ragged for four hours of practice Thursday morning, the last two with Poppy as his partner. It was ridiculous to be so much improved after three classes but facts were facts. Colby was thrilled and didn't hesitate to say so. Personally, Nick knew he was coming along quickly but he wasn't near where he wanted to be.

"Ashleigh, how do you feel about extra homework?" he'd asked.

"For you or for me?"

"Ha. I was thinking we'd meet at my place first, and come here to practice with the others afterward." He needed all the alone time he could get with her to crack her professional shell. Not to mention, it was fun to watch her lust after his pool. He'd be willing to trade a kiss for a dip. Nick was nothing if not persuasive.

Now it was bright and extremely early on a Friday morning and he was back in Ashleigh's clutches. She was as encouraging as ever with her "ONE, two, three"-ing. And he was doing it. One step at a time, but he, Nick Thurston, was waltzing. His pool deck and massive living room passed by in a blur as he saw them from the corner of his eye.

"Chin up," Ashleigh said for the millionth time that morning.

Nick frowned at her as they paused between moves. "I didn't drop my chin this time."

Ashleigh's smile raised more than his chin. "I know." She pulled him into a double combo. "I didn't think you'd notice. If you want to get fancy, we can start running your lines with the music."

One, two, three. "Are you kidding? I'm not ready."

"We've already discussed this. Me teacher, you student."

"Sorry, teach, I think you're wrong."

She stopped in the middle of the floor and stepped back. "I bet you a dollar I'm right. Ask me to dance," Ashleigh instructed.

How the hell did she expect him to ask her to dance? He floundered for a second and Colin Firth's Mr. Darcy popped into his head. Nick didn't want to think about where that memory came from. He stepped forward and bowed slightly at the waist.

Ashleigh curtsied in response, moving as if she were actually were a modest English rose in a floor length gown instead of a kick-ass Cali girl in a t-shirt and sneakers. Visions of old society balls flickered in his head and he could almost hear the band in the corner and a faint waltz beat beyond the buzzing in his ears. Ashleigh held up her hand in invitation. Nick stepped closer until his hand was snugged around her waist and he had a firm grip on her left hand. Ashleigh lifted her chin and, without thinking, he mirrored the action and leaned into her.

They finished the combination and she ordered "again." So he did. His foot barely came down on the final step when she said "turn." He didn't dare break eye contact, concentrating on Ashleigh's next instruction, trusting his feet to be in the right place when they needed to be. She didn't give him any time to think. A minute later they were at the end of the pool deck and he was out of breath. But he hadn't stepped on her toes or stumbled once. "How'd you do that?"

"Me teacher," she started.

"Me student," he finished. "Me very, very grateful student. Holy shit, I did it."

"You sure did. Didn't I say you were ready?"

Nick nodded at her after he finished staring at his shoes. The pride in her big blue eyes made his heart ache a little. She had absolute faith in him and didn't hesitate to show it. She made him proud of himself, doubly so when he knew he'd worked his ass off to earn it. "This is all you."

*

How unexpectedly charming. Not the fact Nick managed to make it the length of the deck. Ashleigh knew what he was capable of. The fact he was so proud of himself for his accomplishment. Unfortunately, they didn't have a lot of time to celebrate. He'd taken the first step, so to speak. Now she needed to ramp it up to get him to performance level.

"Ready to do it again?" Ashleigh asked.

"Absolutely."

"Want to try it to music?"

"Absolutely."

She couldn't help but laugh. "Excellent. Success looks good on you, Nick Thurston." She broke away long enough to set her MP3 player to loop an instrumental version of "Tennessee Waltz", the first song Nick would dance to on stage. She wasn't going to waste time teaching him a single step he didn't need to know.

The gentle strains echoed across the pool. Ashleigh smiled encouragingly and motioned for Nick to ask her again. She had trouble keeping the smile on her face when he pushed right past her frame and tried to yank her close. She stepped back. "No, try again."

It took him two attempts before he was even half as good as their last dance. Ashleigh finally gave him the go-ahead to start dancing and all hell broke loose. There were thrusting groins and roaming hands and a lot of stomping on her toes.

"Stop!"

The hesitant confidence on Nick's face was long gone by the time she called a halt. He scowled at her and she saw his frustrated flush extended well below his unbuttoned shirt collar.

"What was that?" she asked.

"It was supposed to be a waltz," he growled.

"No, what were you doing?" she emphasized. "You did something completely different with me five minutes ago. Is the music throwing you? We can go back to practicing without it."

"I don't see the point, since I need to learn how to do waltz to music and I obviously can't do it the way it's supposed to be done."

"The way it's supposed to be done?" she repeated. What he did was in no way the type of waltz he needed to learn for...Oh. Oh! "Fucking Dancing with the Stars," she spat. The show produced more moron wannabes than every dance movie in the last decade combined and they all seemed to come knocking on her door looking for lessons the week after the season finale.

"Ashleigh?"

"That's what you're talking about, right? A little DWTS action?" She danced around the pool with an imaginary partner, hips swiveling, chest stuck out far enough to nearly topple her. "Nick, technically what they do is a ballroom waltz, but mostly they put on an entertaining spectacle."

"Have you seen their ratings?"

"Yes, and I've seen their costumes. I'm pretty damned sure Poppy isn't going to be wearing a skirt cut up to her crotch and skin-toned mesh holding her tits in place for your 1950's revival. That isn't what you want to be doing."

The frustration in his eyes faded a little and was replaced with confusion which, while better, still wasn't helpful. "I guess I see your point but what we were doing before isn't going to cut it."

"No, it's not," Ashleigh agreed. "But it's a hell of a lot closer. What were you thinking about the first time?" Because she wanted that dance back immediately. When Nick didn't answer, she leaned back to wait. "Spit it out, Nick. I promise not to laugh."

"Jane Austen," he admitted with a sigh.

That was…"Perfect! Yes, that is what we want. Jane Austen dancing is what Otto Blackwood would do at a society ball. A flawless, utterly classy, respectable waltz for everybody to admire while he whispered dirty little suggestions into the ear of the proper young lady he was trying to seduce." At Nick's look, Ashleigh shrugged. "I read the script."

Nick nodded slowly. "Otto would do that."

"Okay, so we'll try it again. No music this time."

He took a moment to pull himself together and Ashleigh couldn't help but picture him in any given Jane Austen story. Lack of sideburns aside, he would fit in. He had the pedigree, the looks, and the class to make all the ladies swoon. With his hair brushing his collar and rakish smile, women would absolutely throw themselves at him a la Mr. Darcy. Ashleigh wasn't immune to his charms. The kiss she was trying to forget popped into the front of her brain in glorious Technicolor. She wasn't sure if she wanted to hug Sydney or smack her for the introduction. As she considered Nick's constant professionalism, Ashleigh leaned toward smack.

"Ready?"

Nick nodded. He dropped into a low bow.

Swoon. She curtsied and Nick stepped up to, but not through, her frame. Great start. He took a breath and led her to the other end of the pool without her giving him a single prompt. He held her gaze and didn't look away once. All she saw were soulful blue-green eyes and a barely there smile as all his focus was on her. It was silent and breathtaking and, for a moment, Ashleigh forgot there was anybody else in the world.

"That was amazing."

Ashleigh shook her head to clear it. "It was. We've done it twice now so there's no going back." She reset her MP3 and recued up the music. "Ready."

They did it again. This time, Ashleigh added a turn at the end. At least, she tried to. Nick was doing well in a straight line; any variation from that and he was back to tripping over his own feet.

"Let's reset and go again."

The turn wasn't happening.

"We'll try again tomorrow. You've done tons today," Ashleigh complimented. She shouldn't have pushed so hard. She didn't mean to erode his confidence.

"Yeah, tomorrow. Honestly, I think my brain is full. Besides, technically I don't need to know how to do a turn. Poppy and I just go from one side of the stage to the other and then stop. I'd rather have that one pass perfect than worry about stuff that isn't necessary."

"Okay," Ashleigh agreed. "We'll get you waltzing in your sleep and then add on."

"Let's do it one more time. I cannot believe I'm dancing. Correctly. I could do this all morning," Nick said gleefully.

Apparently she hadn't damaged his self-confidence

at all. Since he offered, she made them go one last time.

He wasn't stepping on her feet any more but she was suffering a new kind of torture.

Chapter 10

If it weren't for such a good cause, Nick would resent having to beg for a party invitation. At least the guest of honor was a friend of his. It wasn't completely out of the realm of possibility he'd want to celebrate her birthday with her. If Ashleigh happened to be there, so be it.

Nick pointed at his image in the mirror. "You are pathetic." And horny. He was going on forty-eight hours after the kiss-that-could-not-be-named and it was killing him. Damn Ashleigh for being so professional and efficient. If he'd had a week's worth of lessons and hadn't been getting anywhere, he'd fire her and ask her out. But, no, she had to be good at her job and make him learn shit and stuff. Gorgeous, smart, and talented. He'd never been so pissed off at hitting the trifecta before.

He looked back into the mirror, critically this time. He had made time for his highlights and a barbershop shave in the afternoon. His blue-on-blue shirt and tie coordinated with the subtle pinstripe in his slacks. Cufflinks gave him a little bling but if he rolled up his sleeves, he knew Ashleigh would look. She seemed to have a thing for his forearms. He'd primped less for movie premieres.

He owed Chris huge for this opportunity and since he wouldn't have another shot for a year he had to make it count. He wasn't close enough to Sydney to garner an invitation to a small private dinner on his own so he'd talked his costar into hosting a bigger party solely so he could wrangle an invitation. Nick grabbed the small gift bag off the table at the front door and headed to the car.

La Fete was obnoxiously stuffy but they did have the

best French food in the city. Sean Glenn stood talking to the maître d' when he arrived. "What are you doing here?" Nick asked.

"I was invited to Sydney's birthday party," Sean answered, lifting his own gift bag.

"Why?"

"Because we're friends. Why are you here?"

"We're friends." They were, but that wasn't the reason he was here. Sean knew Sydney even less than he did, so she wasn't the reason Sean was here either. But if Sean were willing to let it go, he would, too. Nick was one bad excuse from embarrassing himself and he didn't want to do it in the restaurant lobby.

An elderly tuxedoed waiter quickly led the two of them to a private dining room where half a dozen people were already seated.

Ashleigh was not one of them.

"Damn," Sean muttered under his breath as he scanned the room.

Nick had no idea why his buddy was pissed off. It wasn't like Sean was destined to go home alone, not with all the lovely young women present. He'd surely charm one of them into bed. Sean was famous for it, which was why Nick was surprised to see him immediately start chatting with but not hitting on the stunning black woman in the curve-hugging copper dress. It took Nick a minute to place her. "We met at the volleyball tournament, didn't we?" he asked as he reintroduced himself.

"We did. Good memory. Vanessa Vaughn. Nice to meet you again."

"She's Trent's sister," Sean added.

Now Nick understood the respect. Trent Vaughn was one of the wounded vets they'd met at the tournament. He'd made it clear while the guys could admire his baby sister's volleyball skills, it was all they'd better be admiring.

"Shit, you met my brother? I'm never going to get a date." Vanessa groaned, reaching for her wine.

"I can sympathize," Sean said.

"You can?"

"I have two younger sisters. They didn't date until I left home."

"I'm moving to Antarctica. There are men there, right?" Vanessa asked.

"Syd, can you get Vanessa another glass of wine? I think she needs it."

Nick circulated, kissing the birthday girl on the cheek and slapping Chris on the back. Chris looked tired; movie production schedules could be a bitch. It was good he had two days off in a row. Nick thought Chris had another week of filming left. He was about to ask if he had his timing right when she walked in.

Chris looked past him to the entrance of the dining room. Nick glanced over his shoulder and saw the waiter speaking to the owner of the most delectable backside he'd ever had the good fortune to observe. It was framed by a coral satin dress cinched by a thick belt, and a pair of legs that bottomed out in a pair of silver sandals with three inch heels. The blonde wearing them had a retro hairstyle which put him back in his grandfather's garage lusting after Miss July again. Then he understood his reaction.

The woman turned to toss a brightly wrapped package at Sydney and Nick saw her face for the first time. Ashleigh hadn't looked like that the last time he'd seen her on a night out. By the hard-on he was sporting, his body liked this version, too. He watched Ashleigh see him, focus on him, and stare harshly at Sydney and shake her head. What the hell?

"I'll be right back," Sydney said to Chris.

"Do you know what's going on?" Nick asked.

"Not a clue. And no, I'm not asking. Sydney knows you guys but it was weird enough asking her if I could invite you. I'm not going to start using her as a go-between while you write notes to the girls in the class."

"You guys?" Nick repeated. "Who is Sean after?"

"Nobody. I said nothing. Look, the birthday girl is back!" Chris rushed over to his girlfriend and hurried her to the table.

Ashleigh's eyes looked suspiciously glassy but she blinked and the shine disappeared. "May I escort you to your seat, Ash?" Nick asked.

*

"You've never called me 'Ash' before." She would have remembered hearing those words from his lips. Dammit, he was doing the tongue-lip-touch thing again.

"All your friends call you 'Ash.' We're friends, right? If we were dating, I'd call you 'Miss Jessup', but only if I'd been naughty and you needed to spank me."

"Yes, we're friends. Although you're being a very bad boy right now, Nicholas, flirting like that with a poor, innocent girl like me." This was a disaster in the making. What am I doing? Ashleigh asked herself.

I don't know but I hope it ends with my panties around my ankles, her libido answered. But he's a student, her brain complained.

Don't care, drop panties, her libido argued.

She pictured her brain sighing and giving up. It was a plight of the female condition: a handsome face and all common sense went out the window. Instead of doing the smart thing and running away, she was having dinner with Nick, the actor, not Nick, her student. She was surprised by the difference. In her studio, she was in control of the situation; here, he was.

It was hot.

Not looks-wise. Nick always looked hot. Dressed for clubbing was different than sweaty after a four hour rehearsal but sexy in another way. His confidence was attractive as hell. He was throwing too much innuendo for her to consider him a gentleman but he and Chris were highly entertaining.

She couldn't believe the night was really happening. When she walked into the dining room and saw Nick there, her emotions ran from thrilled to see him to shocked at the situation to betrayed by her best friend in a second and a half. Sydney caught her at the door to the street and grabbed her arm.

"It wasn't me. I swear," Sydney said breathlessly.

"Well I didn't invite him."

"I know. Chris did."

"It's a hell of a way to get around a promise, Syd."

"No, I didn't ask him to. Nick asked Chris to invite him," Sydney explained.

"Why?"

Sydney's "are you a moron?" look could blister paint off a wall. "Because you were coming."

Ashleigh's brain stopped. "What?"

"He likes you, Ashleigh. He really likes you. Since I know for a fact you haven't slept with him, I don't understand why you haven't jumped him yet."

"I don't know. Maybe because," Ashleigh leaned closer and whispered in her friend's ear, "he's my student."

"There is that," Sydney admitted. "But you're both adults and it's nobody's business but yours."

When Ashleigh didn't move, Sydney gave her arm a

tug. "Come back. Have dinner. Flirt a little. You don't have to make any promises. But I am making you keep the one where you said you'd come to my birthday dinner."

Now Ashleigh was eating dinner, having a great time, and finding it much too easy to fall under Nick's charming spell.

"You lie!" Sydney laughed. "Chris, tell me he's lying and you didn't do that to poor Russ."

Chris crossed his heart. "I swear to you the birthday clown-o-gram was charged to Nick's credit card."

"You stole it out of my wallet," Nick countered.

"I'm not admitting anything, but if I were to cross the one guy on the lot who could take on the entire cast singlehandedly, I wouldn't leave a paper trail leading back to me. That's all I'm saying." Chris took another sip of his wine. "God, he was pissed. It was hilarious."

"Did he ever pay you two back?" Ashleigh asked.

He coughed into his napkin. "Actually, I think Sean took the hit for that particular prank."

"I did, thank you very much. But don't feel too bad about it. You'll get yours, Zeusy, and your little god of war, too.

"You had it coming. You rigged our toilet tanks with a bottle of liquid dish detergent. I had bubbles everywhere. For days," Nick told her.

Sydney leaned back in her chair. "Oh my God, that is genius. How does it work?" she asked Sean.

"Why do you want to know?" Chris sounded slightly worried.

"Josh signed me up for the Olive of the Month Club for my birthday. You know I hate olives. He did it so I'd give them to him. I need payback and I'm seeing him next weekend."

Nick leaned over to Ashleigh. "Josh?"

"Her little brother," Ashleigh whispered back.

While Chris attempted to persuade Sydney not to escalate her brother's prank war, Nick stretched his arm over the back of Ashleigh's chair. "How about you? Any family?" he asked

"Not really."

"Too bad. I love having mine in L.A. I mooch dinner off them sometimes."

Ashleigh laughed. See, charming, her libido said. And hot damn is he working that shirt and tie. Too charming. Sydney had to be mistaken; he couldn't possibly be as stuck on their kiss as she was. All she should expect tonight was good company at dinner and a night out in a club she'd never get into on her own. She should be on the prowl for a hunky distraction when they got to Domino; she already had the dress.

"Can I tell you how amazing you look?" Nick whispered as he pulled out her chair after dessert and coffee.

"No woman would say no to that."

"You look incredible." Ashleigh felt his breath on her ear and it sent a shiver down her spine. This was an exceptionally bad idea. She had to work with him. Ashleigh had to call a halt to the flirting before she said something to get her into trouble. More trouble, she corrected herself. If Nick kept it up, she definitely wanted to be in trouble.

She pumped her car's air-conditioning to full blast on the ride to Domino and pulled herself together. Ashleigh held Sydney's hand in a death grip as the redhead tugged her past the line snaking around the corner and through the club door. Then Ashleigh panicked. She was at home in the Jungle. These were not her people.

Her new vintage dress which had been so lovely in the restaurant was now old and used. Her shoes were two and a half years old and might as well have been from the last millennium. Her hair was a joke. Unfortunately Sydney wouldn't let her leave. "Syd, I've got to go. Everybody is staring."

"We walked in with gods from Olympus. They were going to stare. Chin up, chickie, and let 'em drool. We look hot and they're all jealous."

"You and Chris are an item. You have been for months. Everybody loves that the contest winning girl-next-door and the movie star fell for each other. They love you. Yesterday some asshole said I was dating Nick and now I'm getting hate mail."

Sydney's face fell, and the pained, brave smile she used to wear in the burn ward appeared. "Hate mail? You didn't mention that. You can go if you want, Ash. I understand about the stares. I truly do. Thanks for coming to my supper party."

Fuck. Of course Sydney knew about stares. She got enough of them after being caught in a fire which scarred her back and shoulders. If Sydney could hold her head high hearing comments day after day, Ashleigh could be the center of unwanted attention for one night. "I'm in."

It got easier once they pushed past the crowd to a reserved corner on the second level overlooking the dance floor. The company was great and the booze was flowing but before too long, Ashleigh started to twitch. The music was calling to her.

"Do you want to dance?" Nick's voice was at her ear again and she couldn't control the shiver. The shock of his question lasted a second before she beamed at him. She was dying to lose herself in the rhythm and she'd never get the chance to do it with him in Domino again. This was a memory she'd tell her grandchildren about.

"Absolutely."

"Great." Nick waved Sean over. "Sean, do yourself a favor and dance with Ashleigh. She's the only person here who can show you up." He leaned into her again and this time his lips brushed the sensitive skin of her jaw when he spoke. "I know you like to dance and we know I'm not going to be able to do it with you."

Sean Glenn was a huge man and her three-inch sandals didn't do much to match his height but Ashleigh let him lead her through the club. "I honestly do know what I'm doing," he yelled over the music, which had switched to a heavy 90's dance beat.

"We'll see."

Holy hell, the man could move. Nick needed years to become as good as Sean. Ashleigh expected him to be a novice rather than a rank beginner but he knew his way around the dance floor. They felt each other out for the first number and quickly realized they were well matched. When Lou Bega's "Mambo Number Five" started up, Ashleigh's face lit up to match his. "Oh, hell yes!" The tiny area was packed but as Ashleigh and Sean switched from mambo to jive the floor cleared out. Her partner took every advantage of the open space and she was suddenly very glad she'd chosen the outfit she did. Let the other women in the club wear their little size twos; she had the curves for jive and she flaunted them. Her breath came faster as the song played on; the fitted bodice hugged like a glove and the steamy press of bodies had filled the room with a heavy cloud of lust.

Sean spun and Ashleigh moved with him until the music changed. She gave him a quick hug and suddenly Nick was on the floor, picking her up and twirling her around. "Can you teach me to do that?" he shouted in her ear over the applause.

"I'll need more than a month."

"I'm available."

Ashleigh fought back a cough. He wasn't supposed to be flirting! "I need a drink."

She shouldn't be so winded after two songs but she couldn't catch her breath. She coughed again and her ears popped. It took a moment to identify the sound through the wailing music but Ashleigh eventually recognized the fire alarm sounding discordantly over the pounding beat. She tugged on Nick's arm until he turned away from his conversation with Chris. She grabbed both men and yanked them forward.

"We have to get Sydney out of here now," she ordered.

Chris clued in first. He tucked his date against his chest and pushed past everybody between them and the emergency exit. Ashleigh doubted Sydney's feet touched the ground every third step as fast as Chris was moving.

Nick wrapped his arm around her and stayed behind them as the other club patrons began to react. Ashleigh's heel caught on something in the dark, narrow hallway and she rolled on her ankle. She pulled away from Nick as she tried to free her shoe from its invisible binding.

"Go! I'm fine. I'll catch up."

Bodies pushed against her as a sea of humanity moved towards them. She yanked her foot again but the sandal strap refused to give. The press of people grew thicker and somebody elbowed her hard in the ribs. Ashleigh doubled over, gasping. The scent of smoke was noticeable now. Not a false alarm. Thank God Sydney got out. A pair of hands grabbed her arms. "Hold on to me," Nick shouted.

She grabbed a fistful of his shirt up near his open collar as he crouched in front of her. Ashleigh felt his hands around her ankle and she tried to shield his bent body. She doubled over in another cough and almost lost her balance when Nick pulled her foot out of her shoe. Suddenly, she was up in his arms and flying down the hallway.

"Hold on," Nick yelled again.

Ashleigh buried her face in Nick's neck when they burst into the alley behind the club. He continued to hold her tightly even once he had set her back on her feet and she balanced awkwardly on one shoe. "Are you okay? Do we need to get you checked out?" He pointed to ambulances already blocking the street. "The paramedics will have oxygen."

She coughed again. "It's not the smoke. Somebody elbowed me and knocked the wind out of me. Can you see Sydney?"

"She and Chris are over there." Nick pointed across the street to a group huddled on the corner.

"Sean and Vanessa? The others?"

"Are with them. Come on."

She limped her way across four lanes of traffic, holding on to Nick like the lifeline he was. Sydney left her date and grabbed Ashleigh as soon as she was in reach, sobbing uncontrollably. "I couldn't find you. I thought you didn't get out," she wailed.

"I'm out and we're all fine.

Sydney pulled away and hugged Chris again, burying herself in his chest. "Are you really okay?"

"I'm good but I think it's officially time for me to go home. It's after midnight and I lost my shoe." Ashleigh trembled as the situation caught up with her. Fire trucks approached the club from both directions, red lights flashing, sirens off. The club's front doors were closed but Ashleigh didn't see any smoke filtering out from underneath them or from the roof. Hopefully, it was a small fire they'd managed to contain. The firefighters opened the door and charged in, hoses in hand. She didn't see any flames and she breathed a sigh of relief. Maybe they'd gotten lucky.

"I'll drive you," Nick offered. He hadn't let go of her hand, despite the fact she'd almost stopped coughing.

"I'll be fine." Ashleigh covered her mouth as another fit racked her.

"Sure you are. I'll drive anyway. Besides, it's illegal to drive barefoot."

"What about your car?"

"I'll come back for it." Nick leaned in close, his hazel eyes bright and intense. "Ash, let me take you home."

Chapter 11

Ashleigh's fifteen year old Nissan rolled up the street in silence. Nick turned where directed until he was in the parking lot of a three-story walk-up. Ashleigh hadn't spoken during the ride but at least she'd stopped coughing after they'd gone through a late night drive-through and gotten her a bottle of water.

He put the car in park and it sputtered twice after he pulled the key from the ignition. "You need a tune-up," he said, desperate to break the quiet. He understood she was shaken up but her stillness scared him. He hadn't known Ashleigh long but it was wrong for her not to be animated.

"I need a whole new car. Stella has served me well but she deserves to be put out of my misery," she tried to joke. She failed when her voice cracked halfway through.

She went quiet again for a moment. "I have never been so scared in my entire life. I thought they were going to trample me and I was going to burn to death. I couldn't get out of the way. You saved my life, Nick." She reached over and patted his arm. "Thank you."

Nick pulled her hand until she leaned over. Her lips parted and he couldn't look away. He wrapped his hand around the back of Ashleigh's neck and closed the distance.

He didn't kiss her gently. He speared his tongue into her mouth as soon as their lips met and she let him. She nipped at his lower lip and he groaned. She tasted of the chocolate martini she'd been sipping before her dance. The warmth of her mouth threw his whole body into overdrive. He tried to lean closer but his seatbelt yanked him back.

"I knew it would be like that, but fuck me!"

"Me, too. Do you want to come up to my apartment?" Ashleigh slapped her hand over her mouth. "Me, too. Period. New paragraph. Do you want to come up to my apartment to wait for your ride back to your car?"

"Yes, I want to come up." Nick ignored the rest of the statement. She didn't add the qualifier the first time and that was the question he was answering. He very much wanted to go up to her apartment. Kiss her again. Strip her down and get her horizontal. Or vertical–she was flexible.

"Okay."

He was pleased to hear she was as breathless as he felt. She leaned on him probably a little more than she needed to as he walked her to the building door. She led the way up the carpeted stairs and stopped at the door to a corner unit. "I wasn't expecting company," she warned him as she opened the door.

He looked around as she bent to unstrap her remaining shoe. He couldn't have dreamed this. The miniscule apartment was full of character. She had an off-white leather sectional with squishy cushions dominating the living room, and a flat-screen mounted to the wall. Every pillow, every blanket, screamed of softness and comfort and warmth. It was nothing like the strong, practical décor of her office and studio. That was work and this was definitely her home. It was a side of her he hadn't seen before and he liked it.

"Would you like something to drink?"

Hell, no, she wasn't backing away now. Nick shook his head. "What I'd like is to kiss you again."

"I think that's a bad idea, Nick. It was a mistake and I'm not into casual sex."

"Ash, I promise you there would be nothing casual about it." There was no way anything with Ashleigh would be casual. He'd fallen for her brain at the same time as her body. Smart, sexy, confident, successful. If he ever got his hands on her, it would be for the duration.

"So we're talking about dating? I thought we agreed it would be a bad idea," she said.

"I think it's a terrific idea."

"Nick, you just got out of a relationship with your personal dance instructor. How did that work for you? Oh, yeah, disastrously!" she argued.

"Ash, we're both consenting adults. If you can't bend on this, I'll hold off and ask you again when our contract expires but it's won't make a difference to me. Well, the wait might kill me, which would be inconvenient because we could start this journey right here if you're willing to trust me."

He meant it. He would wait if he had to but it might kill him. Technically, blue balls wasn't fatal but by day ten he'd surely wish it were. Nick understood Ashleigh's concerns; he did. But even after a week he knew she was no Sandrine.

"We're on a journey now? First stop, the bedroom?"

Thank fuck. A joke meant she was considering it. "I'm willing to make out on the sofa for a while first," he countered.

"Nick, I'm not kidding."

If she needed convincing, he'd do it. Nick stepped forward and brushed her hair over her shoulders. "Neither am I."

God, she tasted good this time, too. He fumbled with the zipper on her dress when she nipped at his bottom lip again. That trick snapped his control. Nick kicked off his shoes and backed Ashleigh down the hall, never taking his mouth off her. Her mouth, her jaw, her neck. She radiated heat and he reveled in the burn. He found the zipper and they left her dress in a pool of satin on the hallway floor.

Ashleigh's hands pawed at his shirt and her nails scratched his chest as she fought with the buttons. When she grabbed at his belt, he almost lost it in his shorts. He finally let go of her and came up for air. "I've got this."

*

This was a very, very good idea. While Nick dropped his slacks, Ashleigh popped the hooks on her bra and let the straps fall down her arms as she bent to push down her matching panties. Then he was on her again and she fell onto her unmade bed and scooted up the mattress, careful not to break the kiss.

Nick kissed like nobody's business. He hadn't laid a hand on her yet and she was ready to go. Nick pinned her down and smiled. "I'm going to enjoy this," he told her.

He kissed her again, his tongue dominating hers. The force of it made her lips tingle and when he shifted to nibble on her neck, she gasped for air. "Oh my God, Nick."

"We're not nearly there, Ash. Let me get warmed up."

Any warmer and she'd set the sheets on fire. He palmed her breast and pressed her nipple between his finger and thumb hard enough for her to come off the bed. He pushed her back down and moved his hand to her other breast. "Easy, Ash. We're just getting started."

The shock of his pinch shot straight down her spine and had her writhing beneath him, rubbing her thighs together in a desperate attempt for some release. Ashleigh slid her hands up his arms and over his shoulders. "Nick, quit fooling around. Do you want to play or do you want to play?"

"Condom. Shit, my wallet's in my pants."

"Nightstand drawer," Ashleigh instructed.

He leaned over to reach for the handle, putting his chest at a perfect licking level. So she did. She swiped her tongue against his nipple and ran her teeth against his pec. Shit, he tasted good.

"Shit, Ash, do you want me to get this condom on or what?"

"Need help?"

"Sure."

Since he'd asked her so politely to handle his dick, Ashleigh quickly took it in hand. She stroked the hard length of it as she put the condom on. She wrapped her legs around his waist and pulled him down. "What are you waiting for, Nick?"

Nick braced his arms on either side of her and rocked his hips, rubbing his dick against her wet crease. "Don't you know good things come to those who wait?"

"What about very, very bad, dirty things? When do those come?" Ashleigh gasped because, dammit, he was making her crazy.

"Just before you do."

He finally moved. He pushed into her and she was ready for him. Fuck, but this guy was smooth. Nick thrust into her, changing his position a bit each time so every move found a new place to drive her wild. She tried to tell him to slow down and let her have a chance to enjoy it but she couldn't take a breath to speak. He threw her over the abyss and followed her thirty seconds later.

Nick collapsed beside her. "That was incredible but I swear I can do better. Fuck, but did you get me primed, Ash."

He'd taken her from shocky wreck to mind-blowing orgasm in ten minutes and he was apologizing? "I don't think it's possible but you are more than welcome to try."

Chapter 12

It was good to know he could still go all night now that he'd hit thirty. Nick had a quick start the first time with Ashleigh but he was certain he'd made up for it by round three. He might have slept for a few minutes but she'd woken him when she rolled over to turn off her alarm clock. Since he and his dick were both up and awake, he figured he might as well do something about it.

But Ashleigh wasn't settling back into her too small, floral duvet covered, very comfortable mattress. "Ash, what's wrong?"

"Nothing."

"Then come back here."

"I can't. I have to get to work."

"I swear I'll do all the work this time."

She threw herself onto the bed, bouncing perilously close to a part of his anatomy he knew she liked. "You did plenty of work." She bent and gave him a thorough kiss which had him grabbing at her through the sheets, but she pulled away laughing. "I mean it. I have half a dozen five-year-olds who are going to be waiting for me when I open the doors at eight o'clock."

"Tell me you're not serious." Nick wasn't letting her leave the bed unless it was to order in food. He was far too happy here. He'd known Ashleigh was all kinds of hot but he hadn't imagined they would be so incredibly good together. He'd had more than his fair share of women but none of them had fit him physically as well as she had. He didn't know what exactly it was but he didn't intend to let her go until he figured it out.

"I'm sorry. Truly. I have classes from eight straight through 'til three on Saturdays."

She was not doing this. Nick grabbed her arms and flipped her onto her back. "Why are you running?"

"Nick, let me up."

"Talk to me. I told you this wasn't casual and you're trying to rush me out of here like I'm your dirty little secret. You were fine last night. More than fine. What happened?" For what little time he slept, he'd slept well. Nick knew it was Ashleigh, and not her comfortable mattress. They fit in a way he hadn't experienced before.

It wasn't bragging to say he'd worked hard for his success, and he'd have to keep working hard to keep it. He didn't mind hard work but it was nice to come home to somebody who didn't want to discuss his job all day. Ashleigh was interested in his projects but he'd probably had more non-industry conversations in the week he'd known her than he'd had in his last six months of dating. Being with Ashleigh was easy; not effortless, because anything worth having needed to be earned, but the return on what he put in was definitely worthwhile. He wasn't going to let it go without a fight.

"I like you, Nick. A lot. The only thing, the only thing," she emphasized, "I'm holding back on is the risk."

That was insulting. Ashleigh didn't seem to be prejudiced against actors. The tabloids made it look like he was a bit of a player, not as bad as Sean but enough to have his own reputation. "Define risk."

"My business is everything to me. I'm already getting trolled because of the photos of us on those gossip blogs. They're calling me a slut and a home wrecker. I can't afford that kind of continued bad publicity. I can't have a scandal come up when parents run an internet search. We also have the Sandrine problem."

"We've covered that one. I can handle her and her lawsuit," Nick protested.

"I'm good with you handling it but if Sandrine gets stupid and comes after me, I'm screwed. I can't afford another legal battle and her pockets are deeper than mine."

The speed at which she was talking made it perfectly obvious that she was terrified of the thought of going back to court to face off against her former boss again. The facts weren't going to convince her. She had the facts. Ashleigh needed somebody to have her back. From what she had said the night before, she didn't have any family support. Now that he thought about it, it was strange she hadn't mentioned anybody at all. Sydney and Vanessa obviously knew her story because they didn't bring it up. When she said her studio was everything, she wasn't exaggerating.

"I can't stop the press. I'm sorry, but I can't. I can promise if Sandrine breathes a word that comes back on you, I will personally litigate her straight to hell."

"You can't do that."

"I can. If she wants to come at me, I'll deal. If she thinks she has any say whatsoever in my personal life, I'll hire a fleet of lawyers to remind her she doesn't."

Ashleigh relaxed beneath him. She went quiet and still, and it was wrong for the happy, energetic woman he'd come to know. She had a lot of concerns she was handling on her own, and until now he hadn't had a clue. He wondered if her other friends did. She reached to brush a lock of hair out of his eyes and smiled. He returned it. Maybe he was getting through.

"That's sweet but you have enough to worry about with her professionally. I can handle her if she comes after me," she whispered.

"My life is mine. I want you to be part of it and I'll do what it takes to make it happen."

"I'm getting that."

"Finally."

When she smiled, he had to kiss her. Had to. Her lips were warm and inviting. He settled into the vee of her legs and suddenly he was back in high school where he'd make out with a girl for hours, nothing but kissing and some over-the-clothes action. He could do that with Ashleigh but it would definitely lead to some under-the-clothes action. He got to second base before she pulled away.

"Once more to tide us over?" he asked, burying his nose in her hair.

"I want to," she said, "but I've got to have a shower and be out the door in twenty minutes."

Nick wasn't ready to let her go yet. "So what's the plan? For us," he clarified. "You're working 'til three?"

"Uh-huh. I'll be home around four. I don't suppose you'd stick around 'til I get back?" She dropped her head and dragged her hair back and forth across his chest, proving she'd picked up on how much he liked it. "Please?"

"Yes," he agreed. "No. Dammit. I've got an interview at the theater at four."

"Supper?" she suggested.

It was good to know she wanted him to stay as much as he did. Nick shook his head. "I'm having dinner with my parents. Tomorrow?"

"Strategy meeting for the next Curse the Darkness gala with Sydney, Caitlin, and Vanessa in the morning and we've already pushed it twice. Afternoon?"

He had to think for a moment. "I think we're clear. We'll have dinner. Since the last time you looked smoking hot we burned the place down, I'm thinking casual."

She giggled. "I can do casual."

"Thanks for trusting me to stay, but it's not going to be much fun if you're not here," Nick complained, softening it with a smile. "I'll call somebody to pick me up and take me to my car."

She kissed him again. "Do we have a plan?"

"We have a plan."

* * * *

She wasn't purposely dodging Sydney's calls. Ashleigh thought about answering but it was against California state law to talk on a cell phone while driving unless it was hands free. She loved her rusty old Stella, but not enough to drop a whack of cash to get Bluetooth installed in a car half as old as she was.

She tossed two protein bars on her desk and hoped she'd have time to choke them down between the four fifty-minute and two seventy-five minute back to back classes. When Sydney's face appeared on her phone's display after she unlocked the front door and she saw the parking lot was empty, Ashleigh was out of excuses.

"Hello."

"So what happened last night?" Sydney asked without preamble.

"Nick drove me home, which was actually a good idea. I was shakier than I thought. Then he called for a ride to take him back to his car."

"What time was that?" Sydney asked.

"I'm not sure." Technically Ashleigh wasn't lying. She left her apartment a few minutes past seven so it had to have been after that.

"I ask because I went for a drive to clear my head and Nick's car was in the club's parking lot at six this morning. Do you have something to share with the class?"

"No. Yes. We're not discussing me right now. We're talking about you. What do you mean 'to clear your head'? How are you this morning? How'd you sleep?"

"I didn't. And not in the sexy, fun way either."

Ashleigh lost the conversation for a moment, remembering the fun, sexy way she hadn't slept either. She'd had a much better night than her friend. Three times. But this wasn't the time to reminisce.

"Shit, I should have figured. Did you call your therapist?" Reliving your worst nightmare coming true would do that to anybody. How many people got caught in one fire during their lifetime, let alone two?

"Chris made me call first thing. I've got a special Saturday morning appointment."

"That's good. Give Chris a hug for making you call. He's a good man."

"He is. But he didn't sign up for this, Ash. I can't expect him to—"

"Yes, you can. Chris isn't going anywhere. Ask him." Despite his and Sydney's rocky start, Chris was a solid guy who was completely besotted with her friend. The fact it was mutual made them annoyingly adorable together.

Ashleigh heard the tears in Sydney's reply. "He said the same thing," she admitted.

"Bah-dum-dum."

"You are terrible."

"I most certainly am. Do you want me to come over later?" Ashleigh asked. It's not like she had plans with Nick or anything. Dammit.

"No, I think I'm going to lie down for a while before my session. Chris is asleep."

"Okay."

"Not so fast. You haven't told me why Nick's car

was still in the lot at six in the morning. Even after driving you home, he should have picked it up by two o'clock at the very latest. Did you offer him a refreshing beverage? Or something else? I promise not to say anything to Chris."

"You'd better not." But Ashleigh told her. Everything."

Chapter 13

Nick mainlined his third espresso of the morning wondering how members of the press slept at night. He picked up his car and was home before eight and he already had four dozen texts and emails, most of which were from Sean.

It was too early to call considering the lateness of the night before but Nick needed to know what he was facing. He opened the first of Sean's links and pictures of his co-star and Ashleigh dancing dominated the screen. Apparently it had been a slow news night. Rumors abounded about "his girlfriend" Ashleigh abandoning him to dance with Olympus's god of love. Later reports quoted witnesses as saying Sean was the one who carried her out of the blazing building. Gossip blogs ran with it, already predicting a new romance.

He couldn't believe how pissed Sean was about it. "Nick, not that Ashleigh isn't a sweetie but I'm trying to rehabilitate my image as a player. I don't need the internet telling everybody I'm trying to get into your girlfriend's pants."

"What's going on with you? Who are you seeing?" Nick demanded.

"I'm not…Doesn't matter. Are you going to come out about Ashleigh or not? I need to address this now."

"I hadn't planned on announcing my dating habits, Sean, but Ash and I are going out tomorrow night. That ought to answer questions for the tabloids."

"I'll call Layla and see what she suggests for dealing with these assholes."

Nick's head shot up. "Why would you call her?" Layla Andrews, who played Hera on Olympus, had been a common enemy for everybody on the cast for the first two seasons. Last year she'd had some kind of personality turnaround and had worked hard to repair her reputation. It had worked but she wasn't close to her castmates socially. At least, Nick had assumed she wasn't. He had no idea she and Sean were friends.

"Because she's the fucking queen of handling rumors. She's been helping me with other stuff, too," Sean said.

"I had no idea."

"Layla's private. Anyway, thanks. It means a lot to me."

"You'll owe me."

Sean laughed. "Fuck, no. You'll just owe me one less."

"That's fair."

And that was the last thing to go relatively well on Saturday. Brian called to give him shit about getting involved with Ashleigh in light of Sandrine's accusations.

"Brian, you are a fantastic lawyer but nobody gets to dictate my personal life. Sandrine was fired well before I even knew Ashleigh. Now I know her. Can you deal with this or not?" The conversation ended on a chilled note. Supper with his parents was even less enjoyable.

"Who is this girl, Nicholas?" his mother asked over vichyssoise.

Two French meals in two days. His stomach was in hell. "Her name is Ashleigh Jessup. She's a friend of Chris Peck and his girlfriend, Sydney Richardson. She owns a dance studio. She doesn't have any family. She hasn't asked for money, a part, or a meeting with Brian. She's smart and talented and I like her."

"Why isn't she here?" his father asked.

"Because we've been dating a week?"

"If you two were serious, you'd introduce us."

"Mom!"

It went downhill from there.

Fortunately, Italian was the word of the night on Sunday. Nick enjoyed his meal but Ashleigh demolished her appetizer, a huge plate of pasta and a dessert. She warned him when he picked her up that she'd done a six mile run in the morning in addition to working with some private clients for in the afternoon. Nick was exhausted thinking about it. At one point in the evening, he asked her if she wanted to be alone with her vodka penne. He spit out his wine when she shot him the finger. He would have said something but she was so surreptitious about it nobody else saw. That's what made her perfect. Utter class with a bad girl who peeked out every now and again.

"Any problems yesterday with your little ballerinas?"

*

"Still jealous of Tonya and her YouTube twirling video likes?"

"Hey, she may not be a rival today but twenty years from now, she might be the one directing me. Damned straight I pay attention to my competition."

She made him choke on his wine. It was only fair he got her back with her coffee.

She hadn't had any problems with her little ballerinas and tap-dancers. She had problems with their parents, who apparently followed the Hollywood dating scene. After a second mom wandered toward her office while she thought Ashleigh was distracted by a student, Ashleigh dug a key out of her bottom desk drawer. She'd never had to close her office door before, let alone lock it. Emma's mom had the grace to look embarrassed when

Ashleigh caught her but Jacey's mother grumbled loudly on the way out about Ashleigh's "bad attitude." Jacey had two other sisters who took classes. Ashleigh clawed her way through a brief panic attack. She couldn't afford to start losing students over Nick.

She killed time between lessons by working on Nick's routines. She referred to his script constantly as she tried to dance through the dialogue, looking for places to make it easier for him. A dance performance was fundamentally different than a theater one and Ashleigh wasn't confident she was teaching him the right things. He was learning the moves. Using them in a scene was a step beyond.

Ashleigh was wrong when she thought the parents were bad. Her afternoon class started and the teenagers were all over her business. At least four of them took pictures of her with their cell phones and Ashleigh had no doubt they were posted to various sites seconds later. She looked awesome—sweaty, hair everywhere, and in workout clothes which were acceptable but obviously weren't designer. It was exactly how she wanted to be introduced to the world as Nick's girlfriend.

"Girls, phones away now or you'll be explaining to your parents why they have to come to pick them up in person," she ordered. There were more grumbles but they disappeared quickly. The girls unanimously requested she add jive dancing to the program. When she asked why, she was shocked to hear a nearly complete video of her doing "Mambo Number Five" with Sean was online.

At least the fifteen-year-olds were up front about their nosiness. "Miss Jessup, did you really dump Nick Thurston to go out with Sean Glenn?" Hannah, the leader of the pack, asked.

"I am not dating Sean Glenn."

"So it's true you're dating Nick Thurston. He is so hot. What's he like in—" the sophomore continued.

"Hannah, if you finish that question you will be banned from this studio permanently. That is the first and last thing I'm saying about my private life. Are we crystal clear, girls?"

They were clear. They didn't believe her but the questions stopped. From what Ashleigh overheard, they were also planning to get their friends to sign up in hopes of glimpsing Olympic gods on their way to classes. They were doomed to disappointment.

Saturdays were non-stop activity and she couldn't lock the doors quickly enough. She was ready to go when paranoia set in. Ashleigh stared at the SUV at the far end of the lot. Dark windows, hadn't moved in hours, didn't belong to an employee in the strip mall—at least not one she recognized. She was certain she was being staked out. When the dry cleaner owner left at five in his new vehicle, she felt like an idiot. Ashleigh ran to her car before she found another reason to hide in her studio.

Ashleigh took a roundabout route home, paying more attention to her rearview mirror on the drive to her apartment than she had in the previous years combined. She locked herself in her apartment, pulled the curtain, and thanked God Caitlin was on speed dial. "How do you do it? Be famous?" Ashleigh gasped, succumbing to the panic which had been threatening her all day.

"Open some wine. I'll be right over."

She didn't drink wine. She went straight for her bottle of Jack. Caitlin talked her off the ledge while she sorted through Ashleigh's inbox. She did it again on Sunday morning, reporting the number of emails was down eighty percent. Her website hits were up proportionately.

Ashleigh told none of this to Nick. It was her problem and she was dealing with it. All she wanted was a nice time out with him that didn't end in bloodshed or emergency vehicles.

"It was fine. I'm never having teenagers though."

"You don't want kids?" Nick asked.

"Not seven teenage girls at the same time."

"Fair enough."

Nick didn't discuss what was going on at the theater. Work was off the table tonight. Instead there were fierce debates about the state's new proposed eco-legislation, whether or not Scorcese was past his creative prime and the maximum age a couple could visit Disneyland before it got weird.

"There is no maximum age. It's for children of all ages. My grandparents went every other year, and they stopped inviting me once I turned eleven so they were alone," Ashleigh insisted.

"I think it's weird for adults to be there without children."

"It's not. You can sit there and be wrong."

"I'm not wrong," Nick insisted.

"Fine, I'll take you and prove it."

"Fine."

Ha! She could win an argument with Nick. Wait a minute. "You're going to make me take you to Disneyland, aren't you?" she asked.

"After the play ends and before Olympus starts up again? Absolutely."

"Fine. You can be wrong then, too." Her heart tightened a little as she realized his timetable meant he was planning long term.

She must have been wearing her thoughts on her face. Nick called her on it immediately. "I'm kidding.

You don't have to take me to Disneyland."

"You're planning ahead." She tried to explain.

"Yes." He looked at her with concern instead of understanding. He didn't get it.

"You're planning ahead as if I'm going to be in the picture for a while," Ashleigh elaborated. "You barely even know me."

"I know you, Ashleigh." His hand was warm as it wrapped around hers. His thumb brushed the throbbing vein in her wrist. "I've spent every morning with you for a week. I know your work ethic. I know the causes you volunteer for. I know your patience and your humor and your intelligence. I know what your friends think of you. I know you, Ash."

"Well, hell." The man was much too sweet.

"Come on, let's get out of here."

They ended up cruising around, windows open, continuing to offer bits and pieces of their pasts. He backed off the full court press he started in the restaurant and she was glad for it. Everything he said he knew about her was true for him, too. It had been a long time since she'd allowed herself to care when she met a man like him because by the time they reached this point, he'd already lost interest because she was too busy to properly fawn over him.

Nick expected her to be at work six days a week. He was perfectly content to work around both their schedules to get time together. He was scarily perfect.

She took a minute to notice they ended up back at her apartment. "Do you want to come up?" she asked.

"Yes."

But he didn't move.

"Are you going to come up?"

"No."

She frowned. "Why not?"

Nick lifted her hand off her thigh and put it on his crotch. His hard length strained under his slacks. "Believe me, I would like nothing more than to come up and spend the night with you again and I think you'd let me. I don't want to rush this though, and I think tonight has been pretty damn fabulous already but neither of us got a lot of sleep last night and we have to work tomorrow. So I'm thinking, tomorrow, when you come over in the morning, you should bring a bag and leave it at my place. Then you can come back after you're done for the night."

"You are too perfect to be true."

"You were exhausted on Friday night or you would have heard me snoring. So, can I walk you up to your apartment to kiss you good night?"

"Sadist."

"Funny, I've thought the same thing about you."

Nick rubbed her hand against himself a couple more times. "Ash?"

"Yes?"

"Yes, you'll bring over a bag tomorrow?"

"Yes." Absolutely, without a doubt. She'd pack it tonight.

He walked her right to her apartment, came inside, and pushed the door mostly closed, 'til only his fingers which were wrapped around the frame kept it from closing. "What are you doing?" she asked when he caught her by her waistband and pulled her to him.

"If I let go of the door, I'll never get out of here. Kiss me goodnight," Nick ordered.

She liked this, knowing it was her turn to touch. Ashleigh rocked forward slightly and pressed a quick kiss to his lips. She rocked again and caught the corner of his mouth, and again to work her way up his jawline. His cologne was barely there, and she smelled pure Nick underneath it. She moved back to his mouth and stayed there as her hands explored his chest and shoulders and biceps.

"Ash, you're killing me."

"You're the one who turned me down. You can get even tomorrow."

"Trust me, I will."

"Looking forward to it." Then she shut him up again because, damn, he tasted so good.

"Mercy," he said. "I have to go. Have to, don't want to. I'll call you tomorrow." Nick dropped a fast kiss on her forehead and was out the door so fast Ashleigh didn't have a chance to say goodbye.

The anniversary clock on her bookshelf in the living room chimed midnight and Ashleigh realized two things. They'd made out for over twenty minutes at her front door and it barely felt like two. Between her lost shoe on Friday night and her prince-like boyfriend's sudden departure, she was starting to feel like Cinderella.

Ashleigh touched her lips and smiled, even while she locked the door. "I could get used to this princess thing," she whispered to herself.

Chapter 14

"You waltzed me into your pool!" Ashleigh sputtered when she broke the surface. She looked completely stunned. Nick didn't know if he went too far until she burst into giggles.

"And I did it perfectly, without missing a step or looking at my feet," Nick replied.

"How is it possible for you to do that and still not be able to turn?"

Nick shrugged, still grinning. "I started on an angle to make sure you hit the deep end."

"Should I take this to mean you are now confident with your waltzes and we should pair you up with Poppy on stage?" She waded to the edge and waggled her arms at him.

"The ladder is beside you," he said.

"You're not going to help me out?"

"Not with the ladder right there and that look on your face."

"Your momma didn't raise no fool," Nick heard her mutter as she heaved herself to the deck.

He sent her to shower in the pool house. At least he waited until his lesson ended before he'd pranked her. Now he got to look forward to payback, and Ashleigh was creative. Revenge could be fun.

His mother's vengeance, not so much.

"Honey, I'm concerned. You haven't done any research into this girl," she said during her call while Ashleigh got changed.

"What do I need to research? She's fine. She's a good person."

"I'd feel better if you ran a background check on

her."

Nick understood where she was coming from. He'd had more than one girlfriend who dated him for the career benefits she thought he could offer. When he was younger, his mother was quick to spot the parasites for what they were. But he wasn't a kid anymore. Sandrine had simply been the latest and he'd cut her loose as soon as she'd revealed her true motives. "Mom, I can take care of myself. When things get serious, I'll run a check on her but we aren't there yet."

"Nicholas, you fired the premiere choreographer on the west coast and replaced her with your girlfriend. That's not exhibiting good judgment."

"Where, precisely, did you get your information?" he demanded. Her non-response killed any patience he had left. "Shame on you, Mom. Ashleigh and I weren't dating when I hired her. I had to talk her into it. And it wasn't easy. She's not like the others."

Nick ended the call ready to call Russ for a sparring session. He needed to hit something and although he'd be swinging like a madman, Russ would work him into the ground.

Another option was to work out his frustrations in the bedroom with Ashleigh after supper.

He decided to wait.

* * * *

Ashleigh didn't like to think she was the type to revel in schadenfreude but when Jacob James announced his break-up from rehab-famous Tiffany Elders by showing up to an award show on Sunday night with a very pregnant Ami-Marie Jones, who had a new two-carat rock on her finger, she wanted to shout for joy. She thought she'd try to earn back some karma points by sending a check to the neo-natal ward when, early

Monday morning, Brandy Jenkins and Troy Alvarez had announced the premature birth of their twin boys, and the actress/right fielder power couple asked their fans for support. News of her and Nick fell off the front page of every gossip site she checked and her inbox deflated to almost manageable levels.

Now all she had to deal with were her students and Tonya was more interested in talking about her twenty-teen likes on her new video than Ashleigh's love life. Suze nearly peed herself laughing as Ashleigh nodded in intense interest at her daughter's announcement. Her first class of the day went fine. It didn't hurt that she'd already locked her office door.

There were stares and whispers from her other classes but Ashleigh took a breath and set them aside. She was not going to ruin her night with Nick by hanging onto the problems he told her he couldn't fix. Not when she had happy news to share.

She and Nick lounged on the pool deck, watching the lights of LA twinkle below. The Pacific Ocean swallowed all the light from the shore and let the star-strewn night sky disappear into its inky depths in the distance.

"I did it," she told him.

"Did what?"

His fingers tickled her shoulder as he pushed her hair back, exposing her neck. She liked that particular trick. She especially liked when he started nibbling and his lips burned the sensitive skin as he moved down her jawline to her mouth. She almost forgot what she was supposed to tell him.

"I called the realtor for the property we looked at."

He smiled at her broadly. Dammit. It was nice he was interested in what she was saying but he could be interested and kiss her at the same time.

"I thought about it all week. I'm going to go for it. I'm seeing it again tomorrow afternoon and if it looks good, I have a structural engineer lined up."

"You're going to put in an offer? I thought you were looking at leasing the main floor?"

"The building is for sale, too. It was always a possibility but everything about this place works so I'm going all out."

"That's huge. It sounds like we should celebrate."

"It's beyond huge. It's going to be life changing. Literally. If I get the building, I'm going to have to give up my apartment, and I like my apartment. But I'm ready. I can do this. I knew I could do this before, but I've had a couple good things fall into my lap and now I know for certain I can do this." She called it confidence and planning. Her parents had called it blind optimism and wishful thinking. They'd also told her she'd never make a career out of dancing. It was the last thing they'd ever said to her.

"I didn't know I fit into your lap," Nick teased. His hand dropped to her hip and he tugged at her skirt.

"Yes you did. Seriously. I'll have to hire another instructor, which is another expense but it means I I'd have more income, too. I am so excited. Enough shop talk. It's all good and it will keep being good."

"I can be very good. Are you sure you don't want to share the details?"

Ashleigh slid up and down his crotch, the zipper on his jeans biting into the thin scrap of silk between her legs. "I might be tempted to say something. If only my mouth had something else to do."

Nick didn't say a word. He lifted her off the chair and had her upstairs and on his bed in thirty seconds. He shucked his pants and crawled beside her.

"Commando?" Ashleigh asked.

Then her mouth was very busy. Nick moved exactly where she wanted him to; he was incredibly agreeable once she had his dick in her mouth. She flattened her tongue on the tip and sucked hard, spawning a gravelly "Fuck!" from an already groaning Nick. Her lips wrapped around the soft skin, so hard beneath the surface. She took him almost to the breaking point when he pulled away.

"Not that I'm not enjoying myself, Ash, but I've got other plans."

He flipped her to her back. Her top and bra went up and her skirt and undies went down and she shivered when the cool draft from the air-conditioner hit her bare skin. Ashleigh pulled on Nick's arm. "Come warm me up," she whispered.

He was usually one to play but it had been a long time since Saturday morning. She wasn't in any mood to wait either. He slid into her and she spread her legs wider to welcome him. He ground himself into her slowly as she stretched out to get as much full body contact as possible. Then Nick sped up. His body stiffened over hers. She tightened her arms around his back and bent her knees, bracing herself on the mattress.

"I have no control at all with you," Nick gasped. He tensed more, pulling her so tightly against his chest she could barely breathe. But she didn't want to. She liked how breathless he made her, how he filled her and made her feel every stroke. For a man with no control, he had enough to make her lose hers. Her breath came faster as her body raced toward the edge of orgasm. She combed her fingers into his hair and closed her fist. Nick hit the spot and she jerked, pulling hard for a quick second.

"Right there?" He did it again, and when she pulled a second time, she pulled him over, and he pulled her into an orgasm which left her shivering in a way that had nothing to do with the cold.

Since she was already holding his head still, Ashleigh took advantage. God, the boy kissed like a god. She parted his lips and twined her tongue with his. Nipped his lower lip. And lay back when he took over and damn near stole the air from her lungs.

When he collapsed beside her, she rolled against his chest. "Sorry about pulling your hair. I couldn't let go."

"Babe, if I minded I would have said something the first time. Be right back."

He came back with another condom in hand, which he put on the night table beside him. "Planning for round two?" she asked.

"With you there is always a round two."

"Well, I don't have to worry about drive time in the morning so we can sleep in."

"Or get up early for round three." Nick reached out to snag her and dragged her closer. He was a cuddler, and that worked just fine for her.

"I do love a go-getter."

Chapter 15

He wasn't able to convince Ashleigh to make the drive to his place after her evening classes for the rest of the week. They texted each other constantly but the distance was killing him. He had it bad. By Friday, he couldn't take it anymore. Nick was waiting in her apartment parking lot when she got home at the tail end of evening rush hour.

"You look terrible," she said when she noticed him.

"You look perfect."

They were both lying.

Ashleigh looked dog-tired and overheated in the atypical humid LA weather. When Nick included his daily but temporary classes, Ashleigh was pulling back-to-back-to-back fifteen hour days. Even then, she was upbeat and smiling. He got it. He was that way too, even in the middle of a brutal shooting schedule where everything went wrong and nobody could go home until they got it right. When you loved what you did, it wasn't a job, it was a joy.

Nick, on the other hand, had been flying all week. Colby Sinclair was ready to propose marriage to Ashleigh for whipping the cast into shape after his previous disastrous experience with Sandrine. Brian had done his job and Nick hadn't heard a peep from Sandrine all week. The press was leaving him and Ashleigh alone. The stars were aligned in his favor. It was awesome.

Even better was the show's first review. Colby invited a friendly entertainment reporter to a rehearsal and the man loved it. The curtain lifted on "The Last Bachelor" in less than a week and despite how well everything was going, Nick was nervous. The live audience factor terrified him with its unpredictability.

For now, he had the weekend to distract him. He and Ashleigh had tonight, tomorrow afternoon and evening, and all day Sunday. He wasn't thinking further ahead than that. "I come bearing backrubs and Chinese take-out."

It shouldn't be love; they were too new. But the look on her face was awfully close to it and he didn't think it had anything to do with moo goo gai pan. Then her smile dissolved into tears. "Ash, what?"

She held onto him in the middle of the parking lot without a thought. It didn't last long but she gave him a quick squeeze before she let him go. "I really needed somebody to take care of me tonight."

"What happened?"

"I wrote a fifty-thousand dollar check today."

"You went ahead with the building," he said. She hadn't talked about it constantly but he knew it hadn't been far from her mind. When the structural report came in, she'd texted him every time she found something she liked or worried her. Thankfully, all she interrupted was a satellite rugby game from Melbourne. He would have responded even if had been a Sunday NFL day.

"I did. I made the offer. The lawyer and the realtor have the money. It's…terrifying."

"It's fantastic."

After Chinese, and wearing off the Chinese, Ashleigh fidgeted in his arms as they discussed their weekend plans. "What, Ash?"

"Are you sure you want me to go with you to the art show tomorrow evening?

"Of course I want you to come with me."

"But your parents will be there. I'm sure they'd appreciate some quality time with you."

This was adorable. "I had quality time with them last week, and they spent a good part of that time telling me they wanted to meet you." The sentiment was true. Nick chose to use nicer words.

"Why? We've been dating for a week."

She had a point. Nick hadn't introduced most of his girlfriends to his family, mainly because he knew from the beginning they were short-term affairs. It was a hell of a lot of pressure to put on Ashleigh. "If you don't want to come…"

"I'll come. I actually like photography. Just…don't leave me alone with your parents, okay? I don't do parents."

"Okay, I'll be your bodyguard."

"That sounds promising."

If his parents had their way, he'd have one protecting him against Ashleigh, which was ridiculous. His mother hadn't mentioned the background check again but Nick didn't delude himself into thinking the subject was dropped. Besides, Ashleigh showed none of the signs his mom was on guard against. She tried very hard, almost too hard, not to take advantage of him. It was at the point where she didn't ask him for anything. While he didn't want to be treated like a vending machine, Nick wanted her to feel like he was there for her. He had the feeling he needed to search her hidden depths before he found the reasons she was reluctant to ask for even something as simple as a hug.

They decided he'd pick her up at her apartment, giving her time to freshen up after work. She grabbed an apple and a whole wheat bun on the way out the door. Ten minutes later, she said, "We need to hit a drive-through."

"No, we don't," Nick argued.

"Dude, I'm starving. This place isn't going to have food."

"You just ate. And it's an art show. They'll have food," he promised.

"Itty bitty hors d'oeuvres. They aren't going to have enough to feed a woman who's been on her feet all day. Come on, turn, there's a Mickey D's coming...you passed it!"

Nick took his life into his own hands when he laughed out loud at her. "I am not taking my Ferrari through a McDonald's drive-through. I refuse."

She ignored him for a minute and stared out the window. She pointed at an upcoming sign. "White Castle?" she asked hopefully.

"I will get you real food once we're done. I promise." On the up-side, he now had an excuse if he had to leave early. God knew he was going to want to. He'd lied. He had no interest at all in going to an art show. This was about supporting his mom's arts foundation and giving them a quick introduction so he could keep Ashleigh to himself for a while. He liked her but they weren't at the get-to-know-the-parents step yet. A quick face-to-face was more than enough. Ideally they'd be in, out, and seated at a local restaurant in less than an hour.

That plan got shot to hell when he walked through the door of Blue. The gallery spotlighted trendy abstract works, which held no appeal. If asked, Nick liked his art to look like something. He'd survive, though, because tonight the highlights were on the finalists of a local photography competition. There was only so much a person could do to weird-up a photograph.

"Nick? What are you doing here? How'd you know? I can't believe you're here."

"Hi, Benny." Benny Duarte was the show's

unofficial photographer and everybody's favorite puppy dog on set. The young man had become a fixture on set when the studio decided they liked his work on Olympus. "How'd I know what?"

"Aren't you here for the show?"

"The art show. Not the show show. My mom is one of tonight's sponsors. What are you doing here?"

"I'm one of the artists."

"Cool!" It was. Obviously, the studio wouldn't keep him around if he didn't have talent but this was outside acknowledgement. Nick looked for his mother, who was deep in discussion with a guy in a two thousand dollar suit. He wasn't about to interrupt that conversation. "Benny, this is Ashleigh. Would you like to show us your pictures?"

He led them to a six photo display on an interior wall. Half the photographs were of old Hollywood Boulevard, iconic stars and buildings whose patinas reflected the true effects of age on Tinsel town. "Benny, this is good." As in, he'd buy it good. Unfortunately, there were already small stickers beside the information cards on the wall next to the two he really liked. "Congratulations on the sales."

Benny blushed at the praise. "Thanks, Nick. The one on the left took second place in the Authentic Hollywood Exhibition contest."

It was Nick's favorite among the selection. "If that one was second place, I can't imagine the winning photo."

"Want to see it?"

"Is it here?" Ashleigh asked.

"Yes. My girlfriend took it," he bragged.

Benny shuffled them over to a gorgeous young Hispanic woman who was holding court with the youngest attendees in the room. They were dressed in their best but their clothes lacked the designer labels of the older crowd. They were there for her, not the art. Her eyes got big when they hit Nick, and her smile got wider when she saw Ashleigh. "Hi."

"Hey, Rita. This is Nick Thurston. Nick, this is Rita Morales."

"Nice to meet you. You two know each other?"

"She works at my bank," Ashleigh explained to him. Then she turned back to Rita. "Benny told us you won the Hollywood contest. Why didn't you say anything? Show us already" Ashleigh continued.

Nick didn't miss the shooing motion Rita made behind her back. Her friends scattered and she was quickly left alone with the three of them. "Since the contest theme was classic Hollywood, I decided to go with a classic medium."

"Is that a…" Nick leaned closer to the small frame on the wall. "It's a Polaroid. Are you saying this is a recent shot? It has to be. That's you." It was fantastic. Rita had taken a shot of an antiques store window display of seventies furniture, and let the reflection capture her in a brightly patterned polyester mini-dress and high ponytail. The other person in the reflection, the back of a man in a suit, was innocuous enough not to look anachronistic. It looked like a standard 1970's photograph. Except for the Lamborghini from forty years in the future cruising on the street behind her. "Your photo is brilliant."

"Too bad for you, Nicholas, but it's already sold."

"Hi, Mom. I take it you've already met Miss Morales and Mr. Duarte."

"I have and I'm here to let them know the awards ceremony is starting and they need to see Mr. Hill to get ready for it."

As the young couple was swallowed up by the crowd, Nick felt Ashleigh stiffen beside him. Showtime. "Mom, may I present Ashleigh Jessup. Ashleigh, this is my mother, Rebecca St. John."

"Ms. St. John." Ashleigh offered her hand and didn't seem to notice the awkward pause before his mother took it. Or maybe she was simply being a lot more gracious than the woman who'd taught him manners from his very first "cookies, please" request.

"How are you enjoying the show?" his mother asked.

"It's a phenomenal display," Ashleigh said. "Photography is my preferred medium when it comes to art and you have some exceptionally talented photographers here."

"You enjoy the arts? So many of Nick's girlfriends claim to be aficionados. So, photography. Are you acquainted with Ansel Adams?"

Nick swallowed hard as he tried to come up with…anything to change the conversation. Jesus, could his mother be anymore condescending? If the implied insult that Ash wouldn't recognize the potentially most famous American photographer of all times wasn't enough, the saccharine sympathy in her voice made him want to hurl.

"Isn't everybody?" Ashleigh replied with a laugh. Not a real one, but she wasn't trying to fool anybody. "Adams will always be the measurement for American landscapes, especially western ones, and for good reason. Of course, Galen Rowell isn't far behind him. Or ahead, if you prefer color to black and white. Personally I tend to lean toward less structured photographers like Carol Guzy or Keegan Gibbs, which is probably why I agree with Nick on how good the winners are."

Nick picked up on the challenge in Ashleigh's voice. When his mother's posture improved, he knew she had as well. Not one of his previous girlfriends had gone toe-to-toe against his mom and survived. In fact, he wasn't sure if any of them had tried.

"I rather like Guzy myself. If you'll excuse me, we're about to start the presentations." The women smiled politely at each other, teeth hidden, and his mom gave him a quick kiss good-bye.

"Say it fast," Nick murmured under his breath to his smiling but seething date. He braced for the well-deserved onslaught his mother deserved.

Ashleigh took mercy on him. "I don't think she likes me."

He burst out laughing.

*

He laughed at her. Did he not know that was a good way not to get laid? Ever again? Okay, maybe she only held onto her pissed-offedness until he drove his Ferrari into a drive-through and pulled out with a double cheeseburger and fries. She even shared the fries.

That, and the fun with chocolate milkshakes they had later, was the last good memories she had with Nick that weekend. He got called in for a rehearsal on Sunday, ruining the one day off she had. Then she had work, and he had work, and their time together shrunk to their early morning lessons.

All she had to do now was get through this day from hell and get ready for "The Last Bachelor". Nick had tickets set aside for her and Chris and Sydney. Ashleigh thought she'd have to cancel her Thursday night classes for this special occasion but Caitlin had stepped up as a replacement teacher. Ashleigh expected some push back from the parents in light of the recent mumblings but having a special guest instructor who was a professional dancer and who had been cast in movies soothed a lot of self-righteous indignation.

At least one thing was taken care of. The rest of her week at the studio was going to shit.

Summer was always a slow period once school let out. Regular classes stopped, which meant regular income dried up as well. The big year-end recital loomed in two weeks and Ashleigh scrambled for ideas to ensure her students returned in the fall. She usually offered a substantial returning student discount if parents re-registered their kids before the last class.

This year, she had fourteen. Not even fourteen families. Fourteen students in total. Something was fishy but she didn't have a line on it until her little ballerinas spilled the beans.

"I'm going to miss you, Miss Ashleigh," Tonya said, wrapping her little arms around Ashleigh's legs.

"I'll see you next week, sweetie. But I'll miss you 'til then, too."

"No, Miss Ashleigh. After."

"After what, Tonya?"

"My mommy says next year I gotta to go to a new dance school but I like your school better. What if I forget how to twirl? I practice every day but you're the best twirling teaching in the world."

Suze had been one of the parents who hadn't returned any of her emails. Pulling her daughter as a student would be an excellent reason to avoid contact but that was a conversation for grown-ups, not preschoolers. "Tonya, you are my very best twirling student. You can twirl at any school, I promise. Do you want to go grab your knapsack while I talk to your mom?"

"Okay." The little arms hugged her again. "I'll see

you next week. I'll be ready for the recital, I promise. I'll practice extra hard."

The curvy black woman waiting in the chairs by the window tried to avoid her gaze, fussing with the toddler in her lap.

"Hi, Suze. Hi, Andy. I hear I'm losing a student in a couple of weeks."

"It's nothing personal, Ashleigh."

"Can I ask where you're enrolling her?"

Suze shifted her son to her other leg. "I was contacted by another school. She offered six free lessons. That's half a semester, Ashleigh."

Ashleigh scooped a stuffed tiger off the floor and returned it to Andy. She plopped down on the chair beside them. "I'm taking a header here, but I'm guessing 'she' would be Sandrine Gold."

"I can't say," Suze hedged.

"I bet if you do, the offer goes away. Sandrine and I have done this dance before." Ashleigh didn't risk looking at the other woman. She was too furious. Tonya had been her student for two years, and despite the laughs they had at the little girl's antics, she'd been a good teacher. Maybe it was naïve of her to assume there'd be some loyalty.

"I know dance lessons are expensive, Suze. Unfortunately I can't compete with that and keep my doors open. I would really like you to stay with Jessup Dance, though. Is there anything I can offer you to stay?"

"It's a lot of money, Ashleigh."

"It is. As someone who's worked with Sandrine before, I'm going to offer you one small tip. The Sandrine Gold Academy of Dance is a well-respected school with some incredible teachers. That said, I strongly advise you to get pricing for what the second half of the semester is going to cost you. In writing. I think the answer will surprise you. If it does, you have time to register Tonya with me for the fall session at my regular discount."

Suze hadn't flinched but had met her eyes when she said good-bye.

When she spoke to Nick in the mornings, or during their quick chats between classes and rehearsals, she kept her news to herself. He was stressed enough as it was. She didn't want to drag him down with her business problems when she was capable of solving them eventually without his help. She wanted to support him when his big night arrived.

Chapter 16

It was a ridiculous family tradition but Nick wouldn't skip it for the world. He ordered everybody out of his dressing room and locked the door. Then he pulled out his phone and called up his video file. Making sure the volume was high enough for him to hear but not so loud it could be heard in the hall, he pressed play.

The cartoon movie lights came up, the band swelled and the stars came out to play. "Overture, curtain, lights…" the duck and the rabbit sang. The clip was under a minute and Nick grinned the entire time.

His parents had watched the same Looney Tunes cartoon before each of their opening nights. When they'd started, it had been on a private movie reel, and later VHS. But it was a reminder every person had a place on stage and it put him in a good frame of mind. Besides, who didn't love Bugs Bunny? The video ended and Nick turned off his phone and locked it in the make-up table drawer. It was showtime.

He thought he was ready.

*

He had been. The night had been flawless. What a rush! Nick had worked in front of a studio audience a time or two but nothing like this. The energy was electric and powered him through the best performance of his life. When the curtain went down after the cast's encore bow, he thought his heart was going to explode.

A crowd waited for him when he got back to his dressing room: his parents, Brian Alexander, Chris and Sydney, Ashleigh. Jason Ricker and Jessica Smith even hired a sitter for their baby daughter so they could make it to his opening performance. Nick said hello to them all but he saved most of his attention for the handful of specially selected reporters.

"Midas strikes again! That performance was pure gold," Chris shouted as he pounded Nick on the back. "How is it you never ever hit a dud?"

"I'd say luck and pure talent but I think I'd get my ass kicked. Let's say I only work with the best because they make me look good," Nick replied.

Sydney snuck close enough to give him a quick hug and whisper "Great job" in his ear before she eased back to her spot on the wall. Chris patted his back again and they vanished with a promise to see him soon.

Ashleigh gave him a big hug but didn't have a chance to say anything before Brian moved her aside to offer his own congratulations. Nick was thoroughly distracted when he posed with Colby Sinclair and his parents, who were ecstatic about his performance.

"Darling, you were wonderful," his mother exclaimed.

"Great performance, Nick," his dad said.

"Grant was quite enthralled with the lovely actress who played Darla Summers. She did a fine job as well."

"I can introduce you to Poppy later," Nick offered. "Did you say hi to Ashleigh?" His voice trailed off when he realized his girlfriend was no longer in his dressing room. He smiled for more pictures but kept an eye on the door, wondering if she had left for the night or if she had stepped outside for some air.

"Actually, Nick, we had Brian ask her to step out for a few moments. We made sure she understood it was just business," Grant told him quietly with a smile on his lips for the photographers taking shots from the doorway.

"I can't believe you. Did you offer her money to go on her way?" He was thirty years old. In thirty seconds his parents made him feel like he needed a time-out for bad behavior for throwing a tantrum.

"Don't be absurd."

Shit, that wasn't a no. Unfortunately, a second round of photographers and reporters arrived and he had to do the dance again. He sent a small "thank you" up when he spotted Ashleigh again, waiting patiently as he wrapped up his last interview of the night. She was so amazing. His parents weren't totally wrong in what needed to be done but he would have been more polite about it. He couldn't believe he'd hooked up with somebody who was willing to step back when it was necessary to give Nick all the attention when he was on the job. She didn't vanish entirely or go home; she stayed close in case he needed her. He saw a few reporters talk to her, and she replied with brief answers and smiles before pointing them in Nick's direction.

She hovered in the background while he signed autographs for the fans who waited for him by the stage door and he sent her a wink to thank her for her patience. It was a good two hours before he was ready to go. Nick was too pumped to drive. He felt his adrenaline high burning off by the minute, so Ashleigh drove his baby home.

"That was a phenomenal play, Nick. I loved it. It was way better than the videos I saw," she raved. "You may have turned me into a theater fan. It was so much fun! And may I say, as a completely unbiased audience member, your three dance numbers rocked."

"We did rock, didn't we?" He knew they had. Performing in front of an audience with no safety net or retakes was everything he imagined.

"Are we going to celebrate when we get back to your place or are you going to crash on me?" Ashleigh asked.

Sleep? He didn't need sleep. He may never need to sleep again. His brain was racing, replaying the performance, noting scenes to work on for the next night now he knew how the audience reacted.

It was too bad his body couldn't keep up. It was a good thing he took care of Ashleigh first because he was out cold about two minutes after he came. His last thought was how nice it was to come home to somebody who was happy for him without demanding anything back.

* * * *

Ashleigh did the "hurry up" dance in front of Nick's single cup coffee machine. It made good java but it was slow on delivering the caffeine. She yanked the cup off the tray and inserted a new pod immediately.

While Nick's cup brewed, she read the reviews for "The Last Bachelor." A few critics suggested Nick's television background didn't translate well to the stage but since every one of them complimented his chemistry with Poppy, Ashleigh was judging them positive over all. Most importantly for her, there were no negative comments about his dancing skills. Nor about Poppy's. It was an uncredited victory for her which was fine. She'd pass on her names in reviews so long it stayed out of the gossip columns as well.

"Hey, baby, you're up early." Nick bounded into the kitchen, already dressed for a run.

"I was going to bring you up a coffee so you can drink it while you checked out your reviews," Ashleigh explained.

He slipped the phone out of her hand and looked at the screen. "How'd we do?"

"They love you. They love Poppy. They love you and Poppy together. It's a love fest," she happily reported. "Are you going to read them all anyway?"

"You bet."

"Speaking of plays, and in a roundabout way rehearsals, are we going to keep up our morning practices for the rest of your run? You hired me until opening night but we can keep going if you want."

"I'd rather spend the extra time with you."

"Even if your mom hates me?" Oops. That snuck out. She'd studiously ignored the woman's behavior at Nick's premiere, but coupled with their meeting at Blue, her conclusions were unescapable. America's eighties sweetheart Rebecca St. John hated her son's girlfriend.

"She doesn't hate you!"

"I didn't mean to say anything. Please forget it."

He shook his head but his phone rang before his argument got started. "I've got to take this."

"I'm going for a run. Do you want me to wait for you?" she asked. She was shocked to realize she'd been neglecting her running because of the convenience of having a pool at hand. She didn't want Nick thinking she stayed over for anything other than him.

"I wish I could but I have a ton of calls and emails to return. By the way, this discussion isn't over," he said. He pulled her close to kiss her before he disappeared into his living room, coffee cup in hand.

Despite the sunshine coming through the open glass doors, Ashleigh shivered at the little voice in the back of her head that whispered, "Are you sure?"

Chapter 17

Nick was not being defiant or stubborn. Well, maybe he was a little stubborn. But he had more urgent things to do than respond to his father's demands for an audience. He had interviews lined up back to back for days, as well as three more nights of performances before his next day off.

He also didn't think it would be in his best interest to be in the same room as his mother. Aloof was understandable. Downright rude was not acceptable. He understood his mother didn't like Ashleigh, but she could at least fake civility; she was an actress. He looked at the latest notification from his dad and silenced his phone.

"Nick! Nick! Nick!" Poppy jumped him at the front door, squealing in excitement. "Did you see? They love us. LA is fabulous. We would not have gotten this kind of support and press in New York. You are the man."

Responding to rave reviews was a great way to spend the afternoon. Getting random texts and emails from Ashleigh with bits of praise attached added to his good mood. So good, in fact, when his dad texted yet again, Nick decided to call him back.

"Hi, Dad. What's up?"

"Your mother's birthday is next Tuesday."

"I remember." He had an alarm reminder set and everything.

"We wanted to invite you over."

"Dad, I'm working Tuesday. The theater's dark on Mondays." Nick was glad Colby decided to go with the traditional day off. Seven performances a week including a weekend matinee was exhausting. Thank God this was a limited run and not an endless one like Poppy was used to. Nick had no idea how she survived theater long-term.

"I know. That's why we're inviting you over for brunch on Monday. You and Ashleigh."

"I appreciate the gesture but Ashleigh works on Mondays."

"Even in the morning?"

"Not 'til eleven," Nick said.

"We can have an early brunch. She can leave when she has to and you can stay for a while. How does that sound?"

"Great, Dad. Does Mom know you're inviting Ashleigh?"

"Yes and she's looking forward to it."

"Excellent. We'll be there."

And the day kept getting better and better.

* * * *

The week was not ending well. The morning after Nick's opening night, Ashleigh got a call from her lawyer. She'd been expecting to hear from Michiko Takada, preferably with news her offer to purchase was moving ahead. She'd read the inspector's report, made the offer and counter-offer, and now she was waiting to hear back to see if they accepted it. After that, the property transfer would take some time but she requested an immediate move-in date to the empty studio space.

Michiko did not have good news. "Ash, the building's owners are making noises about wanting more money."

"I already upped my offer. I can't go higher. I'm already over budget!" Ashleigh protested.

"They haven't rejected it but they are dodging my calls for more information," Michiko said. "I think, although I'm not sure, they might have received another offer on the property."

"How long can they drag their feet? If they aren't going to sell, I need my money back for another offer." She'd have to start the hunt all over again. It had been a miracle to find a second property she liked. She'd never find a third.

"Fifteen days," Michiko told her.

"Right. I remember that." It's a good thing Michiko gave her the friend and family discount or paying by the hour would break her. She'd forced her friend to explain every section of the purchase offer. "I can live with fifteen days but not one day longer."

"What's the hurry? Sometimes these things take time."

"It can't this time. My lease is up in a little less than three months. If I don't get the building, I'm likely going to have to renew it. I need to know either way. So, please, push hard," Ashleigh explained. She had options; just none she wanted. If the current owners backed out, another year in her current location would build her nest egg even bigger and allow her a new vehicle, so losing it had its up sides.

It would still suck.

When Nick called that afternoon, she didn't breathe a word about the latest development in the disaster that was her professional life. She couldn't bear to bring him down when he was so high about the success of "The Last Bachelor." He'd been worried, more than he mentioned, but everybody loved it. To distract herself from the mindless waiting between classes, she searched for any mention of it and sent him all the links she found, even the silly ones.

She was locking up for the night when she received another call she'd been waiting for. Ashleigh double-checked the call display and answered it with a "Well?"

"It's officially official on paper."

"Fantastic!"

"But not officially official until it's official to everybody else. The announcement's not going out for another week. Sorry."

"For this, I can wait. But I'll be good to go once you are officially official to everybody else? I have time to do something else if you want to change your mind," she offered. But she didn't have to. Her good news stuck and something in her life finally went right. She did a highly unprofessional happy dance all the way to her car.

Chapter 18

Nick did not appreciate the summons. Especially since he was the client. Perhaps it was time to start looking for new representation. Brian Alexander had been part of his family's team since forever but maybe it was time for some new blood. Blood which didn't split loyalties with his parents.

The law firm's receptionist was savvy enough to wave him through without stopping him. Brian, on the other hand, made him wait almost ten minutes. Nick was ready to go for his throat by the time he entered the conference room.

"Nick, we have a problem," the lawyer said.

"What is it?" Nick was not going to lose his temper.

"Miss Jessup has an announcement going up on her webpage advertising she has a testimonial coming from an Olympus star."

Breathe, Nick. He didn't wait to hear more. He had to know. He whipped out his phone and plugged in Ash's business website. Nothing. He scrolled through each page a second time and came up empty again. "Show me."

"It's not up yet," Brian said.

"Then how did you know about it?" Nick demanded. For a moment he'd believed him. His arms trembled as he slipped his phone into his pocket and the only thing that would stop it was holding tightly onto Ashleigh while he begged forgiveness. But she wasn't here and to do that he'd have to admit what he did, or almost did. He had a feeling he knew what her reaction would be. Nuclear.

"One of our investigators informed us it was coming."

"I didn't ask for one of your investigators to look into Ashleigh, or her business, or her website. Which means you hacked her."

"I didn't ask how he got the information," Brian hedged.

Fucking lawyer-speak. "You hacked my girlfriend."

"Things came back on her background check meriting a deeper look."

"I didn't order a background check and you hacked my girlfriend."

"Look, Nick—"

"No, you look, Brian. I'm not Grant and Rebecca's little boy anymore. I'm a client in my own right and this shit stops now. If my parents run a check on my girlfriend, you report it to them. If I ask for one, you report it to me. In this case, I think I can safely assume it's my mother. Also, be fucking sure you invoice her for that investigator and not me."

"Nick, I don't think you realize how serious this is."

"I know exactly how serious this is. If I had any concerns about Ashleigh, I would have come to you. I didn't. Are we going to be able to move forward, or is this going to happen again?"

"I think we're clear." Brian was pissed. The older man puffed up inside his two-thousand dollar suit and glared in a way that used to make Nick apologize for his attitude. Not anymore.

"Fantastic. Have a good day, Brian." One of them should.

Brian was wrong. Had to be. Nick refused to believe Ashleigh would screw him over. She'd been quiet for the past couple days, letting him do most of the talking while he enjoyed the wave of success he was riding. That was supportive, not secretive.

He intended to go straight to the theater but after checking his watch, Nick decided he had time to do what he wanted to do. What he had to do.

No speeding tickets later, because Lady Luck had been smiling down on him, Nick pulled into the dance studio's parking lot. The clock on the dashboard flashed over to five o'clock and he waited for the last two mom-mobiles to leave. He had to knock on the door to get Ashleigh's attention.

He wanted to collapse in relief when she threw herself into his arms. "Nick, what a pleasant surprise! Did we have a date?" She frowned slightly as she looked over his shoulder before she pulled him inside and locked the door again behind him.

"No."

He reached for her and she melted into his arms. He needed her to be as innocent as the look she was wearing. If she wasn't he wanted something to remember her by. He bent his head and pressed his lips against her temple. He moved to her jaw, down to her lips. The warmth of her breath seeped into his lungs, melting the icy lock around his heart. He thrust his tongue deeper into her mouth and she met his enthusiasm with a groan. She slipped her hands into his back pockets and pulled him tight against her. When she rubbed herself against him, he had to stop or he'd take her all the way.

Ashleigh pulled back and smiled at him. "That's a hell of a hello. What's up?"

"I had to see you," Nick sighed. He tugged her over to the loveseat in her office and pulled her into his lap. He needed a moment of quiet to get his thoughts in order. How thankful was he Ashleigh waited patiently for him to regain control? "You were awfully glad to see me? Why's that?"

She kissed him again. This time it was a short, powerful press of lips that left him smiling. "Because I wanted to say thank you from the bottom of my little Olympus fan-girl heart."

Shit. Shit shit shit. He'd been so sure she was different. He grabbed her arms and tried to move her but she refused to budge. "Ashleigh…"

"I mean, I didn't even know you were friends with Layla Andrews. You never mention her, not like you do Chris and Sean. But she called me today and I read the offer she sent and I can definitely do it!"

What. The. Fuck? "Layla contacted you? Why?"

"What do you mean why? You know why, you fantabulous man!"

"I really don't." And he really, really wanted to.

*

This was too weird. Because of Nick, she'd received her first good news in a week and he was feigning ignorance? Normal guys would be shouting the news loud and proud while expecting BJ thank-yous, which she was totally willing to provide. But she'd play.

"The ever-lovely, totally amazing Layla Andrews contacted me today to see if I was available to teach dance to her drama camp this summer. We compared calendars and I'm now hired to teach two full weeks of half-days, which sounds funny but you know what I mean. Since they don't interfere with my scheduled dance camp weeks, it's cash in my pocket because I wasn't doing anything else anyway." She leaned in for another kiss before she popped up and spun around the room. "I love her!"

Ashleigh chanced a look back at the loveseat and saw Nick completely dumbfounded. "Nick? Are you okay? Was it supposed to be a secret? Because she didn't say it was you. I guessed."

He had the strangest look on his face, part sad, mostly happy, and a little bit of something else. "I'm fine, Ash. Congratulations, that is terrific news. I'm so proud of you because you did it all on your own. I didn't say a word to her, I swear."

"Then how did she know about me?"

"It seems you've got fans."

That was an awesome feeling, too. Since she was up, she wanted to stay up, so she held the thought tight to her heart and concentrated on the other thing going right in her life at the moment. "If you didn't come here for that, why'd you come?" she added.

"I've missed you. Two days is too long." Forty-eight hours had felt like forty-eight days. Thank God for the invention of phone sex. It took the edge off but wasn't nearly as good as the real thing.

"I can come to your place tonight if you want. But, honestly, I'll probably be asleep by the time you get home."

"I don't care. I think I need you there. Can you pack for a couple days and stay Sunday night, too?"

"I have work on Monday," she reminded him gently. She was surprised she had to. He was usually good about her schedule, especially since his was now almost in direct counterpoint.

"You don't have any troublesome private clients in the mornings anymore, so you're free 'til eleven, right?"

"Yes."

"My dad is having a birthday brunch for my mom on Monday and they invited you for as long as you can stay," Nick said.

"They invited me? On purpose?" Nick flinched and she realized she'd gone too far. "That is very kind of them, to invite me to a family function when we're so new. Please tell them yes." God, she hoped she was polite enough. She needed to save the rest for when they were face to face because there was no way Rebecca St. John had had a change of heart since Thursday. But she'd do anything to get that look off Nick's face. Fortunately, her last words seemed to do it.

"Thank you. It means a lot. I know you two didn't start off of the same foot but this is a good sign."

Sure it was, if the sign was "Slaughter-this way."

"I'll go home to pack."

"Don't forget your swimsuit. Or, rather, please forget your swim suit so we can skinny dip. I know you love me for my pool," Nick joked, the shadows gone from his eyes.

"Not only for your pool. Just thirty percent or so."

Chapter 19

Thank you, God. Nick cranked the volume of his car speakers and let the bass shake the frame. He knew Ashleigh hadn't done anything underhanded. He knew it in his bones. She had his back the entire time, and he wasn't going to let Brian slip a knife into hers. He waited 'til he was back at the theater before texting Brian "Layla Andrews is A's testimonial." It was petty but it felt good.

Determined to do Ashleigh's teaching justice, Nick grabbed Poppy for a quick practice before the curtain went up. They nailed it again. The curtain rose and dropped and he was four shows down, twenty-six to go.

Ashleigh was right; she was asleep in bed by the time he got home. He had no compunction about waking her. She was on top of the covers wearing a screaming red negligee that hid nothing at all. More importantly, she'd left a note on his bedroom door saying "Wake me!" Who was he to argue with a lady?

Nick peeled off his shirt and threw it on the chair by the window. His pants quickly followed. He looked down at Ashleigh and dropped his hand to his cock. He only needed to give it a couple of strokes before he slipped on the condom Ashleigh thoughtfully left out for him.

He carefully crawled onto the mattress and lay on his side next to Ashleigh. She didn't move. Nick traced his finger from her wrist to her collarbone and snagged the negligee strap. He pulled it over her shoulder. It slipped over her skin, revealing the upper curve of her breast. He did the same to the other side, then pulled the straps lower on her arms until her breasts were entirely free.

The cool breeze of the air conditioner pebbled her nipples and she shivered in the draft. He leaned over and exhaled a warm breath over them. Ashleigh groaned and he got harder. He moved his hand to her hip and tugged the silky material up until he saw the vee of her legs. He pushed his hand between her thighs.

She was already wet.

Nick dropped his mouth to her breast and sucked her nipple between his lips. He slid his fingers into the waiting warmth and Ashleigh opened her eyes.

"Nick," she whimpered, not as a question but as a plea.

She was as ready to go as he was. Nick bit gently on the side of her breast, not even enough to leave a mark but enough to trigger an orgasm which had her clamping around his fingers. She nearly set him off as well.

"Open your legs for me, Ash."

"Please don't stop."

Nick held himself over her and eased into her channel. He squeezed his eyes shut as he concentrated on the sensations from the only place where they touched. "Holy fuck, Ash, you feel so good."

Ashleigh wrapped her arms around him and pulled him closer until they were skin to skin. "So do you." She found his rhythm and she ground her hips into his. "More, Nick. Make me come again."

He gave her harder and faster and suddenly Ashleigh clenched around him without warning. "Oh, God!"

The tightness around his dick was all he needed. Nick pumped away helplessly as his orgasm went on forever. "God, Ash, I don't want to stop." He nearly collapsed on her when he finished but he rolled away at the last second. He kissed her thorough before they both went to clean up.

Ashleigh snuggled up to him under the duvet and fell asleep instantly. He stayed awake a bit longer, enjoying the quiet. Nick never liked falling asleep with anybody before Ashleigh. There were too many chances for someone to sneak a picture of him in bed, and too many of those someones would sell them off to the highest bidder. He didn't worry about that anymore. Nick's last thoughts before the darkness came were of what it would take to make their arrangement permanent.

* * * *

Sundays were for sleeping in and for brunches. Maybe going to church. Although, Ashleigh thought as she cat-stretched on Nick's king-sized mattress, mind-blowing sex was a decent alternative. There were definitely benefits to increasing her commute time. Of course, the commute wouldn't be as bad if she were at her new place of business

She tried not to dwell on the fact Michiko hadn't sent her any updates but Nick's radar went off as soon as her thoughts went there.

"Ash, what's the frown for?"

"I'm having problems securing the new building. The owners are being dicks."

"Can I help?"

"I don't think anybody can help them from being dicks," she joked, "but thanks. Michiko's on it. I'll just have to wait my fifteen days and complain about them being dickish after I have the keys in hand."

"Tell me what you're going to do with it once you have it."

She checked to make sure he was truly interested and wasn't being polite before she launched into her plans, starting with the immediate necessary structural fixes and moving into her apartment tenant goals. She didn't realize he had rental properties until he corrected a few of her assumptions.

"Handsome and smart. How'd I luck out?"

"Sydney," Nick said.

"I definitely owe her."

"I hate to go but I have to leave soon for the matinee performance. What are you doing today?" he asked.

"I am going shopping for a birthday present for your mother. Any hints?" As soon as Nick left, she was calling the recruits, begging help for a successful shopping or die trying mission.

"You don't have to get her anything," Nick said again on his way out the door.

That wasn't worth an answer so she glared at him instead.

"Fine. She likes red."

She should have asked what shade of red. Sydney found an assortment of four inch by four inch painted ceramic tiles with views of the Santa Monica pier, each done by a different artist. The trios were arranged by color palette, offering a choice of a pinkish-red, a reddish-orange, or a reddish-purple.

Ashleigh eliminated the pink one off the top, and sent Nick a text when she fell into a "this one, not that one" cycle. After she settled on the purple ones she was hit with buyer's remorse which lasted through half a serving of nachos and a margarita. Thank God for her girls.

"Be polite but don't kiss her ass," Caitlin said. "Nobody will respect you, especially you. We have to kiss enough ass on the job. Homes should be ass-kissing-free zones."

"Unless…" Sydney's voice trailed off as she smirked.

"TMI!" Caitlin and Ashleigh shouted in unison.

Sydney raised her glass. "So are we celebrating or

not?"

"Not me, not yet," Ashleigh said. They forced her to elaborate about the new building and its associated problems, which is why she brought it up in the first place. She needed to vent and she wasn't comfortable doing it to Nick. Sometimes, his eyebrows came down for a second when she mentioned something going wrong during her day and she wasn't sure why. But she'd only known him for a couple of weeks. Easier mood reading would come with time.

After she related the news from Michiko, Caitlin slumped in her chair. "I do not like the sound of that. It gives me a bad vibe."

"You don't get vibes. Ever." It was something the three women had in common: all facts and logic, no flakey decisions allowed in the judgment process.

"Okay, I made a poor word choice. I have no proof but I find the timing on this to be highly suspect and I can't put my finger on why at the moment. What about your lease? Are you going to renew?" Caitlin asked.

"I have to let them know at the end of the month, so it will be tight with the fifteen day wait. Maybe I should see if they are open to extend my current lease by a month before I have to renew," Ashleigh said.

"Couldn't hurt," Caitlin agreed.

"Yes, it could," Sydney argued. "You don't want to tell your leasing agent you're thinking of getting out before you have to. I vote for running down the clock. I agree with Ashleigh. I smell anchovies." The other women stared at her. "It's a metaphor for smelling something fishy."

"Conspiracy theorists unite," Ashleigh offered as an alternative toast.

"That, I'll drink to," Caitlin agreed.

"What? You won't celebrate either?" Sydney asked.

The black-haired actress shook her head. "Not 'til my news can't be taken back."

"We're going to have to try this again in a month," Sydney said.

Caitlin and Ashleigh stared at each other for a second before answering, "We're in."

Chapter 20

Nick glanced to the driver's seat and sighed. There were women who didn't care if they made an impression, women who wanted to make a good impression but didn't want to appear they were trying hard, and women who wanted it known they were trying. Today, Ashleigh fell into the third camp, and it bothered him. She shouldn't have to try so hard. Yes, she'd give his mother a well-deserved smack-down at Blue but she'd done it politely. More politely than he would have been if the situation had been reversed. Now she was afraid that his mother hated her and nothing he said calmed her down. He told her brunch would be a casual affair, and what she'd selected from the four wardrobe changes she'd brought over was the most put-together casual outfit he'd ever scene.

"Please relax," he said. "You're making me nervous."

"Why are you nervous? She likes you." But she eased her white knuckle grip on the steering wheel long enough to reach over and give his thigh a squeeze.

"Higher," he ordered.

Ashleigh laughed and the tension in the car dropped by half. Thank fuck. He desperately wanted to tell her she was overreacting but she might not be. His mom had taken a dislike to her and he had no idea why. If there had been anything else in the investigator's report, Brian would have hit him with it at their meeting.

They took her car so she could leave for work when she had to. Nick would call his car service or beg a ride from his parents after the brunch, especially if he decided to hang around for a while. If they made it to the house at all.

"One moment, please, while I check with the house."

Nick leaned across Ashleigh's lap and stuck his face in the window. "Robert, it's me."

"I have orders to check," the guard insisted.

"Since when am I on the check list?"

"It's not you, it's your guest."

Ashleigh sucked in a breath and pinched her lips together so tightly they turned white. "Make your call," she said.

Nick slipped his hand onto her thigh, prepared for her to push it away immediately. Instead, she held onto it like a lifeline. When he tried to speak, she squeezed his fingers and shook her head slightly. Five painful minutes later, the guard let them pass, refusing to look them in the eye. Nick couldn't tell if the man was embarrassed by his and his employer's behavior or if he was scared spitless of the look on Ashleigh's face. Nick didn't care enough to ask or trust himself to speak.

He directed Ashleigh to a parking spot which allowed a quick getaway. He had the feeling she'd need it. "We can leave. I'll say you had to go to your studio early for something," Nick offered.

Ashleigh shook her head again. "I was invited to this party and I'm going to be a polite guest and wish your mother a happy birthday and give her the gift I brought for her. If she's changed her mind and wants me to leave, she can tell me herself. I want to make a good impression for your family but I'm not about to kiss her ass."

Her stance was more than fair at this point. Nick held her hand while they walked to the door. Rather than risking another long wait while his mother made Ashleigh's welcome known, he used his key and they walked straight in.

"We're here," he called.

"On the deck," his father answered.

"If you like my pool, you are going to go crazy for this one. I come over to swim sometimes. They have a waterfall," he said.

"Really?" A smile cracked her pale face. "That sounds nice."

Nick wasn't surprised to see Brian at the breakfast table. He was practically family. The other couple, a man and woman in their early fifties, were unexpected.

Grant Thurston's face revealed nothing. He greeted them with a neutral smile and returned to his coffee. Rebecca St. John rose to meet them. "Nicholas, I'm so glad you were able join us. Hello, Ashleigh."

"Happy birthday, Ms. St. John." Right, because his mother hadn't asked Ashleigh to call her Rebecca, and Ashleigh knew it. Ashleigh stepped forward with the gift bag but Rebecca didn't move to accept it. Ashleigh set it on the glass tabletop beside her and stepped back.

He recognized the spark in his mother's eyes but he didn't know how to protect Ashleigh other than to remove her from the situation. He also knew Ashleigh wasn't going to run. He was fucked.

"I thought I'd make it a family affair to give us all a chance to get to know each other," his mom continued. "Nick, have you met Heidi and Thomas Jessup? Ashleigh's parents?"

What? No. Ashleigh told him they were dead. But when he looked at her, she wasn't surprised at the introduction. She reached for his hand again but this time when she squeezed it, he didn't squeeze back.

"Tom. Heidi," she said, her voice colder and flatter than he'd ever heard it.

Her mother approached them first. Nick noticed

Ashleigh shared her mother's blonde hair and blue eyes but favored her father when it came to her height and strong build. Heidi moved to hug Ashleigh but was blocked when her daughter stuck out her hand for a handshake. "You look well," Ashleigh said.

"Is that all you have to say to me?"

Ashleigh pursed her lips together. "Yes."

"Rebecca says you told Nick we were dead," Heidi said. "I'm so disappointed."

"We're both used to that. Why are you here?"

"The Thurstons contacted us to let us know you were dating their son. They invited us to help us reunite after you said such hateful things about your own family," Thomas said.

"Did they offer you money? Because I know you're not here for me."

Nick watched in amazement as Ashleigh turned away from them. What the ever-loving fuck was going on with his girlfriend? He couldn't believe he'd been so wrong about her. Obviously her parents weren't dead if she was keeping up with their professional lives.

"Please excuse me for a moment. Nick, can you please show me where the powder room is?"

Powder room. How fitting, considering she'd ground his trust to dust.

*

"I told you my parents were dead? When did I ever mention them?" she growled as soon as they were around the corner. Ashleigh sucked in the air she hadn't been able to find when she walked into the ambush at the pool. Her stiff muscles began to shake as the shock and adrenaline hit her. She'd hurt tomorrow; being that tense was equivalent to being beaten in a workout.

"You said they were dead. The night of Sydney's

birthday party. I asked about your parents and you said they were dead," Nick shouted back.

Think, Ashleigh. She closed her eyes and replayed the conversation in her head as accurately as she could. "You moron. You asked me if I had any family around and I said not really. You jumped from that to dead all by yourself."

"It's the same thing. You let me think you were an orphan!"

"How could I possibly have guessed you were so off base? I never said 'dead.' My friends, who you've met, never told you my folks were dead. You must have gotten that impression from all the questions you asked me about them. Oh, yeah, you haven't asked me one single thing about my family."

"I was being polite. I didn't want to broach a painful topic."

"Polite? If you thought I was an orphan, why didn't I even get an 'I'm sorry your parents are dead' from you? I know why. Because you're a self-centered asshole who didn't want to expend energy anywhere outside the bedroom," she shot back.

A sharp cough sounded behind them. Ashleigh turned to see Rebecca St. John standing down the corridor. Ashleigh wouldn't quite categorize the look the woman wore on the deck as a smirk. Now it was even less of one but she wouldn't classify it as a smile. "I think there's been some confusion. Perhaps you two could join us outside again."

Ashleigh tasted blood as she bit back her response. "No, thank you. I think it would be best if I left." As if she'd risk going out there and showing her face again now that she didn't even have Nick to watch her back anymore. Thank God she'd brought her own car. "I wish you a happy birthday, Ms. St. John, but I can't picture further conversations going any better than this one."

Rebecca St. John motioned down the hall. "Please," she repeated.

Ashleigh followed her out, head held high. She hadn't done one single thing wrong in this scenario, and she'd be damned if she was going to act like she was sorry for anything. All eyes were on Nick's mother when she reappeared. "I apologize to you and Ashleigh. It seems there was a communication error. She never told Nick you were dead."

"How gratifying," her father sniped. "What did you tell him? Are you back on that abandonment story? Are you still telling people we kicked you out because you didn't want to go to law school?" Her dad looked at Nick and Grant Thurston as he continued his self-excusing rant. "We supported her through her first degree, even though you lied to us about what you were studying. I don't think it's unreasonable we expected her to support herself after that if she didn't want to come into the family business."

"Ashleigh was always difficult." Her mother picked up the familiar tale. "We wanted to support her artistic career but it's hard enough when you're the best of the best, and she's not. Ashleigh was a solid B+ student but that's not good enough, especially when a dancer is her size—too tall, too heavy. At some point, as a parent you have to tell your child the truth and we did repeatedly but she never listened. Ashleigh was never going to break into the entertainment business as a professional dancer. We told her she'd be on her own until she gave up her ridiculous dreams and we'd be happy to discuss a new arrangement when she wanted a real career. She hasn't had any contact with us since."

"That's me, the perpetual disappointment. Of course, the 'no contact' isn't true, is it, Heidi? Well, it's true on your side." She'd spent twenty-one years as their daughter when she graduated from college. She knew they wouldn't change their minds without proof to convince them she hadn't made a mistake. So Ashleigh sent Mother's Day and Father's Day cards and birthday and Christmas cards full of letters and clippings of her successes as one of Sandrine's instructors. Then she sent an invitation to the opening of her own studio, hoping that kind of success would heal the breach. She held her breath when she mailed an invitation to Jessup Dance Studio's first anniversary recital. When there was no response, she knew it would never be enough. She stopped with the extras and simply mailed cards with her name at the bottom.

Nick's mother definitely wasn't smiling now. Airing other people's dirty linen was never comfortable, especially if you were in the wrong. She'd go so far to say Rebecca looked uncomfortable but Ashleigh was beyond caring. "I hope this answers any questions you have about my background to your satisfaction." She knew, knew, she'd never be good enough for that woman's son, just like she was never good enough as Heidi and Tom's daughter.

Chapter 21

Between a rock and a hard place didn't cut it. Did he chase after his girlfriend whom he accused of lying to him, or let her go and defend her against two sets of parents who were actually telling lies about her? Nick hesitated too long. Ashleigh must have sprinted for the car once she cleared the front door because she was at the gate by the time he was outside. The guard opened the gate as she approached, probably thinking his mother sent her packing. Which she had.

Nick returned to the deck where the previously united guests now sat in an awkward silence drinking coffee. "Well, that was fun. Thanks for arranging your birthday entertainment, Mom."

His father pushed away from the table. "Nick, let's have a chat."

"That sounds like a great idea. Mom, enjoy your guests."

His dad's office was on the main floor, tucked behind the living room. The clean glass and steel furnishings reflected the man's straightforward way of doing business. If someone threw bullshit Grant Thurston's way, he dealt with it and them without mercy. It was why he was working on his third long-running series of his career. "Don't blame your mother."

"Don't cover for her. We both know you would have handled this another way. Like, oh, talking to me or to Ash about it. Not by blindsiding her."

The older man rubbed his face with his hands. "That girl has plans for you, Nick. If you had only talked to Brian…"

They were not turning this around on him. "I did talk

to Brian. The testimonial he was talking about? As soon as I left Brian's office I went to ask her about it, as a grown-up does. She greeted me at the door all excited Layla Andrews had offered her a contract to teach dance at her theater camp. Ash thanked me for arranging it, which was very thoughtful except I didn't do it. Why? Was there more?"

"What about gaining sympathy lying about her parents being dead?"

"That was me. I misunderstood and I didn't follow through. Although, after meeting them, I don't blame her for acting like they're dead. Calling her fat and untalented to her face? Fuck, what assholes. You heard them. It's not the first time they've done it."

"It was…unfortunate."

"This entire situation is unfortunate. Why do you hate Ashleigh so much? You don't even know her. This is way beyond your normal paranoia." Nick watched a flush steal up his father's neck. "Dad?"

"Your mother got a call from Sandrine Gold, apologizing for her presumptions and asking Rebecca to play peacemaker between the two of you. Rebecca was unimpressed but Sandrine begged her to, if not help her, to help you. She went into detail regarding her history with Ashleigh. Your new girlfriend isn't afraid of using some pretty nasty tricks, Nick."

"Neither is my old one. Ashleigh told me about both sides of the situation. In detail. I assume you used what was in Brian's report as confirmation for what Sandrine told you. How long have you had your report on her anyway? Mom's been a bitch to her since the art show."

"We wanted to see if you'd come to your senses without interference," his dad tried to explain. "Nick, you aren't new at this. You should have had Brian run a background check on her at the beginning."

"To discover what? That she hasn't lied to me? I would have run it when we got serious. Now I know there's nothing to find but we might not have the chance to get serious." Thank God he hadn't confronted Ashleigh about her upcoming web post. She solved that problem without even knowing it and he wasn't stupid enough to bring it up again now it had been laid to rest. She'd probably forgive him for the background check since he had nothing to do with it. Forgiving him for calling her a liar was a much shakier proposition.

Yes, her phrasing had been ambiguous but it didn't excuse him for not asking her about her childhood. She was right; he had been self-centered. Now that he knew about it, he was even more impressed with her than ever. His parents had smoothed out most of the stones in his path when he said he wanted to go into the family business and it had still been a hard climb. He couldn't imagine doing it without their support, let alone with them trying to knock him down all the time.

"Can we have her number? I think we should call her to apologize."

"Dad, truthfully, I think she'll let it go to voicemail and delete it without listening to it, and I don't blame her. Let me try to talk to her first. If she's willing to forgive me, I'll ask her if she'll accept an apology from you and Mom. But it had better be good, especially from Mom, because this was fucking brutal."

"Thanks, son."

It was an uneasy peace but Nick felt confident it would hold, at least on his dad's part. He needed to have a chat with his mother.

Which would apparently have to wait. The breakfast table was deserted when they returned. Nick grabbed a glass of orange juice and some smoked salmon on toast before he strode through the house to find her. He lurked in the hall as she finished showing the Jessups the door.

She held up a hand to stifle any comment he wanted to make, and snagged his glass as she walked by. She refilled it as soon as she got to the table and threw herself into the lounger by the pool. "Please don't say anything for a bit, Nick. I'm too busy kicking my own ass to give you a turn at the moment."

"I'll wait."

"Do you know what they said while you were gone? They admitted Ashleigh had been in contact with them but since she hadn't apologized for her behavior properly they weren't going to reward her with their attention. They did exactly what she said they'd do."

"They asked for money?" He'd heard Ashleigh's accusation but he hadn't taken it literally. He was going to be groveling for days.

"Close enough. They said Brian's firm did good contract work but he lacked specialization in tax law. They said all this in front of him. Then they invited us to move our accounts to keep it in the family in case Ashleigh did manage to 'hook you.' That poor girl. Nick, I'm sorry."

The wind picked up, lifting a sheet of tissue paper out of the gift bag Ashleigh left on the table and slapping it into his mother face. Shit. He was pissed off but he didn't need to rub salt in the wound. "Mom, let me take that."

She beat him to it. She pulled the rest of the tissues out and lifted the small, heavy package from the bottom of the bag. The framed painted tiles brought a wry smile to her face. "She's very good. Smart. Gracious in the face of adversity. And able to twist the knife with a smile on her face. This would have been an excellent olive branch and I turned it into a 'fuck you' to myself and she wasn't even in the building. I think I approve of this girl."

"I'm glad you approve of her. Now I have to get her to approve of you. It may take a while." Nick reached for a fresh glass. "So, while I wait for a car to take me back to my place, what's the name of your florist? The one who you say turns sucking up into a floral art form?"

* * * *

She thought her Monday couldn't get worse. Showed what she knew.

Ashleigh had messages from Michiko Takada waiting for her on her office voicemail. Six of them. She was still reeling when Michiko called for the seventh time that morning.

"Ashleigh, I am so, so sorry. I don't know what happened."

Tears burned in her eyes. "Do we know who outbid me?" She'd lost the building after the owners refused her counter-offer. At this point she should go back to bed and try again tomorrow although with her luck the mattress would spontaneously combust with her in it.

"I could find out. Do you want to make another counter-offer?"

"I can't afford to make another one." Her original offer had already been at the limits of her budget. As badly as she wanted a new studio, she wasn't going to bankrupt herself to get it. Maybe it was a sign she wasn't ready for the big time. "If they've rejected my offer, can you get my deposit back quickly?"

"Absolutely. It's the law."

At least that was on her side. "Well, shit. It looks like Jessup Dance Studio is staying here for another year." She might have the time but she didn't have the energy to go on another property hunt. She was done. The month had started with so much potential and now it was one blow after another. Even Nick had revealed his true face and it was ugly.

"If you change your mind, let me know."

Ashleigh's printer hummed to life. "Are you faxing confirmation I didn't get the building right now?"

Dead air greeted her on the phone. "I haven't sent you anything."

The machine spit out a second page. Then a third. Ashleigh picked up the first page to start reading it and got as far as the first paragraph. "Motherfucking sonovabitch asshole jerkwads!"

"Ash?"

It wasn't possible. It was legal but it was impossible. "Royal Leasing has informed me they will not be renewing my lease. I'm out of here in ten weeks whether I like it or not."

"What the fuck?" Michiko shouted.

Ashleigh grabbed at the rest of the papers and scanned them quickly. "The cover letter is the official part. They attached a personal note at the end saying I was a great tenant but they had an offer from a dance school that was expanding and was willing to pay premium rent for my location."

Ashleigh listened to a "click-click, click-click" sound coming over the phone, the sound of a ballpoint pen in the hands of someone with too much energy. "That is the same reason the other lawyer gave me for the sellers backing out of the deal."

A single name came to mind. "It's Sandrine Gold. She'd trying to close me down again."

"You don't know for sure."

"Oh, yes, I do," Ashleigh insisted.

"Okay, you can't make accusations like that in public or she will hammer you, and we both know she's drunk enough Kool-Aid to try it."

Fuck it. Fuck Sandrine and the leasing company and the building owners and her parents and Nick's parents. And Nick too for that matter. His crimes were less severe but she was feeling pre-emptive. "I'm going to have my real estate agent send me every listing they've got. These fuckers are not taking me down."

"There's the ass-kicking Ashleigh we all know and love." Michiko laughed. "Let me know the minute you want to make a move. I'll lock the deal down so tight Houdini couldn't get out of it."

"I'll call you."

Ashleigh scrubbed the hot tears off her cheeks. Her parents hadn't broken her before and she wasn't going to let them do it now. She might add some more cracks and chips to the collection but she knew who her friends were and they were more than enough.

Chapter 22

The bouquet was gigantic, more than big enough to express three apologies in one vase. Nick needed his Escalade to transport it. He waited until the kiddy class left before he hefted it out of the back and lugged it across the parking lot.

"Delivery!" he yelled as he kicked at the doorframe.

Ashleigh wore the same smile she'd given him that night in the Jungle. The polite one meant for strangers. "Those look lovely. Can you bring them into my office?"

If she offered him a tip after he set them down, he was going to kiss the attitude right out of her, apology first be damned. Nick found a space among the piles of shredded paper on her blotter. "Are you making confetti?"

"Yep. I made copies first but I had to work out my frustrations."

"Bad news?" He was stalling and he knew it.

"I'm fine."

In the Freaked-out, Insecure, Neurotic, and Emotional sense maybe but in no way was she fine. "Want to talk?"

"No thanks."

He didn't blame her. He wouldn't share with somebody who'd been an asshole either. "Can I talk? I need to apologize."

"Go ahead."

His mother was right. Gracious and good with a knife. "I had no idea my parents would look up your parents based on a comment I made. I didn't know your parents were going to be there and on behalf of my parents, I'm sorry you were ambushed like that. As for myself, I'm sorry I accused you of lying about them. You're right. You never once said they were dead. I assumed and I was wrong. I'm sorry I haven't asked you more about yourself. It was selfish and thoughtless and it won't happen again." There. That was as straightforward and honest as it got. Ashleigh could accept his apology or not.

"I'm a lot of things, Nick. Some of them uncomplimentary. But I have no idea why you assumed 'liar' was one of them. I've never lied to you, except for the part about hoping your mother has a nice birthday. After this morning, I hope it sucks."

"She feels terrible," Nick offered. Yep, he was more than willing to throw his mother under the bus after that horror show. "She wants to apologize, if you're willing to hear her out. Your parents said a few things after you left that pretty much explained why they aren't in your life."

Ashleigh snorted. "Big fucking surprise there. I've been able to recite the 'our daughter is a disappointment' speech from memory since I was ten."

She hadn't told him to get out, so he kept going. "How did you get them to pay for degree in dance? Based on what I've seen, I can't imagine them agreeing to it."

"Hence the double major. Business is a fine background for a law degree. They tolerated me taking a dance minor in case I wanted to debase myself and go into entertainment law. I overloaded my schedule and paid for the extra credits on my own to get my major."

Nick had seriously underestimated the woman in front of him. She didn't need to lie to get what she wanted, from him or anybody else. She just went out and took it. "I'm really very sorry, Ash."

"Do you have any more questions for me? I'm not going to play this game again considering I shouldn't have had to play it in the first place."

"I have tons of questions for you. But I'll ask them rather than assume I know the answers. Okay?"

"Okay. I accept your apology." She leaned over to smell the bouquet, then settled behind the desk, shifting the flowers out of the way. "Can you stay for a while?"

Should he go around the desk and kiss her, or would that be pushing it? He sat in one of the guest chairs. "A little bit. What's with the confetti?"

"A couple of fax notifications. I was outbid on the building I put an offer on and my landlords informed me they've rented this space to somebody new and won't be renewing my lease."

He needed a moment to process her casual words. "You're homeless?"

"In ten weeks."

"When did you find out?"

"This morning."

"You need a do-over for today."

She smiled at him, a real one. "Never look back, you're not going that way. I could use something to look forward to, though."

Excellent. He knew he was right to hold off on the kiss. "I can do that. I'm helpful that way."

"Then get over here and be helpful."

*

She was so damn easy. Flowers, an apology, and she was good to go. The facts they were gorgeous flowers and it was a full-assed apology didn't hurt. Besides, she believed him. He came to her carefully, as if he were unsure of her reaction, so she gave him a hint. Ashleigh leaned forward and placed a hand on either side of his face.

They'd had hot and they'd had slow but they'd never

had tentative. She probed at his lips with her tongue and they parted slightly. He kissed her back gently and pulled away. "That was a little awkward."

"Maybe we're both a little upset." He lifted her out of her chair and shuffled them back to the sofa where he pulled her into his lap. He pulled her in close until she snuggled to a more comfortable position against his chest. "Did your landlords say why they aren't renewing your lease?"

"Another dance studio has made an offer for the space and they're offering nearly twice what I'm currently paying for rent. They're willing to let me stay if I match it," Ashleigh said. Nick made a good pillow.

"What about the building? I thought the sale was pretty much done."

"Another dance studio has made an offer for the space and they're offering a lot more than I did."

His arms tensed around her and his heart beat a fast tattoo under her cheek. The hand rubbing circles on her back stilled. "What are the odds there are two completely separate unknown dance studios at work here?" he asked.

"Slim to none. Now I don't know for a fact it was Sandrine but if it is she'd better have deep pockets to pay for all this new property." Looking past the PITA factor, Ashleigh took some perverse pleasure in how much Sandrine was willing to spend to mess with her. She was apparently worth a shitload of time and money to aggravate. She felt special.

"That's harassment."

"Not legally. I checked."

Nick's hand started up again. "So what are you going to do?" His voice was a little off. It had an edge to it she didn't recognize. He wasn't pissed off at her; she knew that tone. This was different, concern and…something.

"I looked at another property, almost identical to this one but a bit bigger. If it's available, I'll take it, even if the rent is stupid. In the meantime I'll keep looking."

"Nothing keeps you down for long, does it?"

"Nope. Life's too short as it is. I'm not going to let someone else make me lie down and die." They were brave words but every time she took a hit, it was a little harder to get up again. Each time she pieced her heart back together after somebody stomped on it, it lost a little bit of the spark that made her Ashleigh and left her a little more fragile. She always ended up on her feet but the reasons why she should bother were getting harder to find.

"Do you want to go out for lunch?"

Ashleigh looked at the clock on the wall. Lunch would be good although she'd prefer to stay and cuddle. Unfortunately, she didn't have time for either. "I can't. I have a private lesson in ten minutes."

"Okay, I'll go. Will you come to my house tonight? Please?"

"Yes."

The cuddle helped because their goodbye kiss was much better than their make-up kiss. Nick's hand down her yoga pants didn't hurt either. The buzzer on the back door rang before they got any further. Ashleigh let him out the front door and raced to the rear of the studio to let in her clients.

The goofballs were wearing matching blinding yellow t-shirts with black smiley faces and flaming red yoga pants. Ashleigh didn't even know they made red yoga pants. "Did you two get dressed in the dark?"

"This is the costume for the video."

Ashleigh tried to laugh but she was too horrified to make a sound. "Please tell me you're joking. Where did you even...I don't want to know. For the love of God, tell me you have something else to wear during rehearsal. I'm going blind here."

Her sight returned as the women peeled off t-shirts to reveal their real workout clothes underneath. An hour later, they put them back on since their sports bras were dripping sweat. "I think we're set for filming. Caitlin, this is your show. Do you want to make any changes?"

Caitlin shook her head. "We're good. I'm happy and the boys will be happy. Any problems with the schedules?" Twin head shakes answered her. "Okay, we're on for Friday. I'll bring the costumes and fax you the times and locations tomorrow."

At least that part of her business was on track.

Chapter 23

Ashleigh was pulling away and he couldn't blame her. He may have regained a little ground with the cuddle session but he still felt the distance. Nick didn't have much time but he squeezed a few minutes out of his schedule for a couple of phone calls to try to help her out. The first was to Brian to see what the legal repercussions would be to make an offer on property with the intention of backing out at the last minute on some excuse. There was no way Sandrine could afford to expand into two new properties at the same time in the same neighborhood. It made no sense; the area couldn't support two new studios on top of Ashleigh's established one.

The second was to his mother. "The good news is she liked the flowers, accepted my apology, and my balls are intact. The bad news is you are the least of her problems right now and she's unlikely to give you a second to apologize until she gets some other stuff sorted out first."

"What kind of stuff?" his mom asked.

"She's looking for new studio space and she keeps getting outbid and undercut by a rival."

"I recognize your tone, Nick. Business is business. Ashleigh seems to understand that. What's got your shorts in such a knot?"

His mother exuded class but the people who truly knew her never forgot she was the third of four daughters of a North Dakota farming family. "Sandrine Gold is the one messing with her."

"It's actually a compliment to Ashleigh if Sandrine Gold sees her as such serious competition."

"I think the line between competition and harassment is about to be crossed and I can't protect Ashleigh. I've asked Brian to look into it."

"Did she ask you to?"

"No, Mom, she didn't ask me for anything. Are we back here again?" Wow, their truce lasted for a whole two hours.

"That's not what I meant, Nicholas. It's great to be supportive but involving yourself in her business without an invitation is not a good idea. If she says she's handling the situation, let her handle it."

"It's my fault Sandrine is targeting her in the first place." If he hadn't broken up with Sandrine and hired Ashleigh, Sandrine would never have re-entered her life. He wouldn't have entered Ashleigh's life either and since that wasn't something he regretted it was up to him to make it right. "I'll fix it for her."

"Nick, learn from my example. Don't assume things about Ashleigh Jessup. Talk to her before you do anything. She's a smart cookie. You don't want to start tromping around making a mess when she already has a plan to deal with this in play."

"Okay, Mom, I hear you." He heard her but he had no intention of leaving Ashleigh to clean up his mess on her own. It was his fault; fortunately he knew just how to fix it.

His third call was to his financial advisor. If Sandrine outbid Ashleigh on that building, he should be able to outbid her. It was a solid property according to the inspector's report and he was always looking for new investments. Besides, he already had a tenant lined up for the main floor.

When his planner, his realtor, and Brian all gave him shit about his seat-of-the-pants rescue-Ashleigh plan, he should have caught a clue.

*   *   *   *

Ashleigh felt rich. Having a fifty-thousand dollar check delivered did that to a person. Yes, it was already her money but that wasn't the point. Her offer was officially rejected and she was back in the market. She could take her official check to the bank for cash money if she wanted to take a few bundles of bills home and roll around on the mattress on them. She wasn't certain if it was more of a rock star or a Scrooge McDuck maneuver but it would be fun to do it once.

She grabbed the envelope from the courier and ran it to the bank in between classes to redeposit it. She heaved a sigh of relief as the figures in her account balance jumped off the anemic line they'd been riding. Having it to roll around on was great but she needed something to spend it on. About two thousand square feet or so of something.

Before she did the math to figure out exactly how many one dollar bills she'd need to fill a wading pool, Caitlin called with even more good news. "It's officially official. Mike Mosley and I are now full-time cast members on Olympus. The announcement went out this morning."

"Yay, Caitlin! Now can we celebrate?"

"Absolutely. Are you busy tonight?"

She had time for a drink before she drove to Nick's place. He was going to be home late anyway. "Sure. I'll swing by the apartment." She finally had something to celebrate. At least Caitlin's timing was good. Michiko called as her after-school classes started, so she reluctantly let the call go to voicemail.

Five hours later, she collapsed on her office sofa and put her cell phone on speaker so she didn't have to expend any energy holding it up to her ear. "Ash, you are not going to believe this. The Duncan Building is available again. The financing fell through. The listing agent called me directly since you were already interested and they're desperate. Do you want it?"

"Yes!" Ashleigh shouted. Then she realized she was answering her voicemail. It was too late for Michiko to do anything for her tonight so she carefully saved the message. She wouldn't need a reminder on her phone to call as soon as the sun was up the next morning.

She was dog-tired. The day-long emotional rollercoaster accentuated the physical exertion of a full day of dance. Her ass dragged as she locked the studio door. Ashleigh's heart got a jumpstart from the metallic screech and the crunch of breaking glass behind her. Motherfucker. Holly Parker, her dry-cleaning neighbor's just-licensed daughter, had taken off her passenger side door mirror and creased her side panels from door to bumper. Poor Stella was barely limping along as she was. Ashleigh didn't know if this recent damage would push her into "not worth the repair money" territory. She didn't have a choice; a new building would wipe out her car fund.

She spent an hour she didn't have to spare exchanging insurance information and calling in reports. Then she got caught in a traffic jam that took over two hours to clear. Thank God she'd peed before she left the studio and had skipped her slushie stop, otherwise her bladder would have exploded. She opened the car windows, turned off the ignition and texted Caitlin and Nick updates. "On the 101." "Still on the 101." "Haven't moved." She and Stella rolled into her apartment parking lot well after one.

She didn't wait 'til she was inside before she dialed.

"Nick?"

"You're not coming over." He said it as a statement, not a question.

"I'm sorry. I just got home. I'm not pissed or dodging you, I swear. I'm exhausted."

"Are you up for phone sex," he teased.

"Do you find snoring sexy?" she countered.

"I'm disappointed but I get it. You've had a hell of a day. This might be a good thing. I'm working on something and this way I'll be able to surprise you with it."

"You don't have to do anything. We're okay."

"I want to."

She didn't have the energy to get into it with him. "Thank you. Shall we try again tomorrow?"

"Definitely."

"Okay, tomorrow."

Nick hesitated before his good-bye. It was the perfect place for an "I love you" but she held off, mostly because Nick hadn't said anything.

What was she going to do when he did?

Chapter 24

Why was it so hard to do the right thing? Nick spent four hours on the phone attempting to get all the pieces in order but he wasn't ready to pull the trigger. He didn't understand. It was a commercial building, not the Taj Mahal.

At noon, he gave up. If he kept bothering his people, they were going to turn on him like rabid weasels. He'd deserve it. He gave them an impossible task and he knew miracles couldn't be rushed. Nick's stomach rumbled as Chris slid into his passenger seat.

"Where do you want to have lunch?"

"Sean's place," Chris said. "We need to make plans to properly welcome our new castmates."

A good round of prank planning was just what the doctor ordered. Also, Sean knew how to cook. "Sounds good."

Nick hadn't been to Sean's new place. The high-rise condo building was a few blocks from the beach. The guys checked out the down home furniture in his living room and parked themselves on the sofa, which was much more comfortable than it looked while Sean joined the conversation from the kitchen.

"What are we going to do to Mike?" Sean asked. "More importantly, who are we going to pin it on?"

"Do you want to rig his toilet with liquid soap?" Chris asked. "That was a good one."

Sean shook his head. "No, I hate repeating myself."

"Bribe wardrobe to shorten his toga to a mini-dress?" Nick asked.

"Bedazzle his sandals?" Chris suggested. He threw up his hands at the looks they gave him. "I wouldn't do it.

I'd get Sydney to."

"Replace his script for the table read? Kill him in the first scene?" Nick threw out.

"Oh, I've got it. I've so got it!" Sean said.

Damn, the boy was evil. Genius, but evil. It would take some doing and some cooperation between the cast and crew but it would be epic. That brought them to Caitlin.

"Come on, man, you've got to have some ideas on how to get Caitlin," Nick said.

"I blew my wad on my Mosley idea. I don't think we can pull it off on both of them. You guys will have to come up Caitlin's on your own."

Something didn't sit right. Sean always had a suggestion; it's what made pranking him so hard. His retribution was exponentially more imaginative than anything they came up with on their own. "You're hot for Caitlin, aren't you? You don't want to ruin your chances!" Nick laughed.

"I didn't say that."

"You just did."

Nick never wasted ammunition. He and Chris needled Sean mercilessly even as he served them a meal of spiced beef and lettuce wraps but Sean held firm in his denials.

When he pulled out his phone to post welcome messages to the new actors, it beeped with an incoming text from Sandrine. The message was short. "I apologized. She's not going to. In fact, she'll deny it. I tried to warn you." It beeped again when an alert for a post from Ashleigh appeared. He clicked the alert first. And then again with a text from his father.

"What?" Chris asked.

"Nothing." All his girlfriend was doing was using his

damn name and reputation as advertising for her business. "I'm very excited to announce actor testimonials coming tomorrow from Olympus and the hit play The Last Bachelor," he read aloud. "That's not horrible." He was willing to do that. He would have like to been asked but he'd told her she'd done a great job. If he didn't give her one, he was certain Colby would. In fact, he didn't know whether or not Ashleigh and Colby had already spoken.

Then he went back and clicked his dad's message. "Motherfucker!"

"Nick, what?" Chris asked.

"My dad says he just spent ten minutes listening to Ashleigh pitch all the reasons he should hire her as a consultant on his show."

"Wow, that's tacky," Sean said from the kitchen.

It was but Nick wasn't upset about it. To be upset, he'd have to care and he didn't anymore. After everything he'd done for Ashleigh, she was just another gold-digger. He was buying her a building, for fuck's sake. And she wanted more? "I've got to go. Sean, can you give Chris a lift? Thanks."

"Nick! I don't think—"

The slamming front door cut off the rest of Sean's protest. Of course he'd try to defend Ashleigh if he was trying to get into her friend's pants. She lied to him. Layla Andrews, his ass. It was a cute cover but the truth was out. Now she was going to admit it.

* * * *

Her friends were great. Michiko had been waiting for her call the next morning. She even had the paperwork ready for Ashleigh to sign. Ashleigh got dressed and swung by her friend's office before breakfast. She wasn't letting the Duncan Building slip by for anything. She'd come too close last time and had already done all her prep work. This time she made the offer with one significant change. It was take it or leave it. She wasn't giving them a waiting period or leaving them any wiggle room. If they were as motivated to sell as Michiko thought, her move should work in her favor.

Now she needed to hit the bank. Again. She called ahead to have Rita start the paperwork and was in and out with another check in minutes. She made another trip to Michiko's office. After that she treated herself to a black coffee and lemon loaf slice, the breakfast of real estate champions. It had been a perfect morning so far, with the promise of Nick later. It couldn't be better.

"Oh, fuck me," she complained to the universe. Rebecca St. John was waiting in her parking lot. There was no way to avoid her so Ashleigh met her number one fan head on. "Good morning, Ms. St. John."

"Good morning, Ashleigh. Won't you please call me Rebecca?"

That wasn't how she expected this conversation to start. "Would you like to come in?" Because of her early start, she had an hour and a half before her first class. She'd have more than enough time to put the studio back together if things got out of hand.

They moved into Ashleigh's office, where Rebecca refused Ashleigh's offer to make coffee and settled for a bottled water. "This is a wonderful space. I love the Dirty Dancing poster especially. I almost had a chance to work with Patrick once. God, he was a gorgeous man. I've always regretted not getting the role."

It was before her time but Ashleigh had to agree. Dirty Dancing was one of the hottest dance movies ever made. "I'm not sure how to agree with you without accidentally insulting your husband."

Rebecca laughed like Ashleigh said the funniest thing she'd ever heard. "Nick was so right about you. You don't believe in beating around the bush, do you?"

"Not really. I'm told it's a character flaw."

"It's not. It's a refreshing trait. Unfortunately, it's not one I often see in Los Angeles and I didn't recognize it at first." The older woman reached across the sofa and grabbed Ashleigh's hand. "I am very sorry about my behavior. It was atrocious and undeserved. I hope you'll forgive me."

The problem with apologies, Ashleigh thought, was when they were sincere you felt like a shit when you didn't accept them. Even if you didn't want to. Especially when you didn't want to. She had every right to carry a grudge, but a grudge plus guilt would get burdensome very quickly. "Thank you."

"I'm used to protecting my son. I've been doing it his whole life. But he was right. Nick's an adult now and I have to trust his opinion, especially since his judgment of you has been much better than mine has been."

"Thank you again."

"I hope you've forgiven him about yesterday morning. He had no idea what was coming." A frown line creased Rebecca's forehead. "He was mad and he didn't hesitate to let me hear about it either."

"We're good. Better," Ashleigh corrected. "He came to see me with flowers." She gestured at the gigantic bouquet on the corner of her desk. "We straightened out the not-an-orphan thing." Rebecca wanted honesty? She'd give it to her. "It was a hell of a bump though."

"If you and Nick have moved past it, I hope we can, too."

Ashleigh's ringing phone broke the awkward silence. She excused herself and went into the main room. She answered it with a desperate "Be good news."

Michiko said three words that had Ashleigh doing a one-woman conga line through her studio. "I just bought a build-ing! I just bought a build-ing!" When she ended the call with promises to send a courier to pick up even more paperwork, she turned to find Nick's mother leaning against her office door.

"I take it your call was good news."

"The best news. Fresh coffee worthy news. Would you like to go next door to get a cup with me?" Rebecca St. John wasn't her ideal celebration partner but she was there and Ashleigh felt an olive branch was due. Ashleigh spilled the beans on her new studio, in infinitesimal detail, starting with the first time she saw it all the way to this morning's offer and acceptance. She tried to rein back her enthusiasm but Rebecca kept pressing her for more details.

"What's wrong with your current place?" she asked.

"It's too small. I've pretty much grown out of it and I have plans to expand even further. I'm getting some fantastic referrals from a couple of girlfriends. Not to mention, my landlords have already leased the space to somebody else."

"You canceled your lease before you knew you had the building? I don't know if you're courageously ballsy or…" Rebecca trailed off, seemingly realizing any word she used would be insulting.

"Breathtakingly stupid?" Ashleigh finished for her. "Neither, I'm afraid. It wasn't my decision. They decided not to renew my lease after they were contacted by another dance studio which wanted the space and was willing to pay to get it."

"I thought you said that's what happened to the other building you bid on?"

Ashleigh smiled into her coffee cup. "It is."

Rebecca pressed her lips together, sealing off any comment she might want to make. Eventually she said, "Do you know the name of these dance studios?"

"No. I've made assumptions."

Rebecca fell silent again. "The file we got on you contained copies of your legal issues. I'd have the same assumptions. Do you intend to take any action?"

Ashleigh nodded. "I intend to laugh my ass off watching whoever it was try to get out of a two-year lease and back out of an accepted offer to purchase. I'll add pointing to the laughing if I can keep my purchase under my hat for a few days. I'm not saying I might say something desperate sounding online to spur further action on their part but it sure would be fun."

Rebecca's phone rang and she took the call. "Hello, Grant." Ashleigh watched a shocked look flash across her face before she waved an "it's okay" sign. "No, Ashleigh and I have been chatting and having coffee for the last hour." She nodded along to a conversation Ashleigh couldn't hear. "Yes, I think you should. I'll talk to you later."

Ashleigh looked up to the squeal of tires in the parking lot. "I think Nick just pulled up. Do you mind if I pop out for a moment and invite him to join us?"

She sped across the parking lot as he pounded on the studio door. "Nick, guess what I did?"

"I know exactly what you did." His scowl froze her in her tracks and his icy words cut to the bone. "Sandrine was right about you."

Totally. Wrong. Reaction.

Chapter 25

Ashleigh looked pissed off at him. Why was she angry? He wasn't the one who was in the relationship in order to use her name. "I thought we had an understanding about using each other professionally."

"Okay. What does that have to do with me being like Sandrine?"

Great, now she was playing innocent. She did it well; he'd fallen for it so far. "She warned me you'd find a way to manipulate me when I came to you for dance lessons. I didn't believe her because I didn't think anyone could use me as badly as she did but you managed to. My dad?"

"What about your dad? What are you talking about?"

"I'm talking about you using me as a testimonial for your business. I'm talking about you calling my dad and using use our relationship as the basis to force him to hire you."

He watched as realization swept across her face. She knew she was busted. "You think I want to use you as one of my testimonials? I'm pretty sure we already had this conversation. If you have a question for me, you ask it. And I have no idea why you think I asked your dad for a job," Ashleigh shouted.

"Okay, Ash, I have a question for you. When were you going to ask for permission to use my name?"

Her voice was so cool it gave him goose bumps. "Thanks for asking, Nick," she replied calmly. All her previous anger vanished. "The answer to your question would be never. Besides, you don't get veto rights on what I put on my website."

"I'll bet you had a good laugh when you told me about Layla Andrews and her summer camp."

A flicker of a frown crossed her face. "That was almost two weeks ago. I hadn't even made any announcements at that point. Why are you bringing that up?"

"I'm bringing it up because you were going to announce an Olympus actor even back then and you lied about it not being me."

"It was never you. I don't owe you any more explanation than that. But you do owe me one about this supposed conversation with your father. What is going on? And keep in mind this is your last chance."

"Are you denying that you called my dad to ask him to hire you as a consultant for his show?"

"Yes, I'm denying it."

She didn't flinch. She lied straight to his face. Nick would rather that she put a knife right through his heart. "How do you sleep at night?"

"With a clear conscience."

She was serious. Her cold blue eyes sparked but she didn't look away. She didn't think she'd done anything wrong. Nick was done with her. He'd had enough lies and manipulations to last him a lifetime. "I can't believe you almost had me buy a building for you. Did you know I tried to outbid Sandrine? I was going to rent you the space you needed so you'd have a place to move. Thank God it didn't work out. I guess you'll have to find a new sugar daddy."

"Had you buy a building for me? Fuck you, Nick. I never asked for your help and I don't need it."

What an ungrateful bitch. "Make sure my name stays off your website or you'll be hearing from Brian. You were such a mistake. Everybody saw it but me. I would have been better off sticking with Sandrine."

Finally something got a response. He should have

gone after her professionalism from the beginning since she didn't have any shame on the personal front. Nick didn't flinch as Ashleigh dashed tears away from her cheeks.

"I wish you two all the happiness you deserve. Now get the hell out of my face."

He let her have the last word since it was the last thing she'd ever get from him. The Ferrari's tires squealed as he sped out of the parking lot, determined to get as far from her as quickly as he could.

Ashleigh had the power to push him over the edge and make sure he was crushed by the fall. How had he let her get so close in a month? He needed to clear his head and figure out how she'd managed to slip beneath the defenses he'd been honing since he was a kid.

He glanced at his cell phone when it rang, determined to ignore it. Sandrine's face flashed on the screen.

On the other hand, misery loved company.

* * * *

"My son is a moron."

Ashleigh turned to find Rebecca standing behind her, leaning against her car. She scrubbed away more tears, not able to speak yet. What happened? How had she gone from celebrating a new building to losing her boyfriend in five minutes? She hadn't done anything wrong! Ashleigh had no idea what he was accusing her of. She never intended to use her relationship with Nick for anything but him. Where was he getting all this crap?

Rebecca held up the coffees she'd grabbed off the table. "What do you say we move this inside? Do you have alcohol?" the woman asked.

She nodded yes to both questions. It took three tries to get the key in the lock, and two more to twist the deadbolt to lock the door again. Her hands were shaking so hard she almost dropped her keychain.

"How much did you hear?" she asked.

"I got there when Nick asked when you were going to ask permission to use his name on your website. I recognized that look as soon as I saw his face. I knew it was going to get ugly."

"Why are you still here?" She was a little ruder than she intended but the idea behind it remained. Why hadn't Rebecca St. John gone after the son she'd been protecting the day before?

"You just finished telling me a couple of your girlfriends were going to help you with publicity for your new studio. Did using Nick's name ever even cross your mind?"

"No, he's not a dancer." Oops. That came out completely wrong. It should have been two separate sentences. "No, I never considered it. If he offered a testimonial I'd take it but he isn't a dancer so his endorsement wouldn't carry as much weight as I could get from other people."

Rebecca loved her answer. "That's an understatement. But you wouldn't have asked even if he was a dancer, would you?"

"No. I'm not—I mean, I wasn't dating him for a referral. I didn't even want to date him in the first place while I was working with him. He's the one who said we were adults and didn't have to worry about compromising my professionalism." The truth burned off most of the hurt and left some righteous indignation in its place. This whole situation was on him. "Your son is an asshole."

"What was he talking about, buying a building?"

"I have no idea. I didn't tell him about the Duncan building. I didn't know it was back on the market until late last night." On what planet would buying a building for somebody without talking to them first be a good idea? She didn't even have a chance to tell him she'd solved her problem on her own, and that her patience in failing to jump to Sandrine's tune had netted her an even better space.

"And I didn't call your husband for a job. I don't even have his phone number." Her tears started up again as she realized her latest round of good fortune had been exceptional, and had been balanced with equally bad luck. She'd been right before. Successes in her professional life always caused losses in her personal one. She needed to stop trying to have both.

"I'm going to go. I'm very sorry, Ashleigh."

"Don't say anything to Nick about being here. Please?" Nothing good would come of further involving his mother and Ashleigh thought of a dozen ways it would make things worse.

Rebecca St. John exhibited her well-known grace as she left Ashleigh to fall apart in her office. She gave herself an hour, leaving herself enough time to have a cold shower to minimize the swelling around her red eyes and to jumpstart her brain again.

Falling to pieces after getting heart-stomped was allowed. Staying that way wasn't. Ashleigh was tougher than that; she'd proved it more than once. She'd survive this, too. No matter how much she didn't want to.

Chapter 26

One, two, three. One, two three. Ashleigh was a horrible girlfriend but she did teach him how to waltz. He and Poppy danced across the stage, flirting outrageously, much to the audience's delight. Their run was half-over and Nick continued to get totally jazzed from every performance although he missed having somebody to share it with. He missed Ashleigh's cheerleading and support, even when she was only listening to him. She made him feel like the most important person in the room, always. At least, she had.

A knock on his dressing room door roused him before he fell too far down the Ashleigh-regret rabbit-hole. "It's open."

Poppy Travis popped her head into the room. "My fridge died and all my water is warm. Do you have a spare cold bottle?"

"Help yourself." He noticed her favoring her left leg as she pulled two bottles from the mini-fridge and tossed one to him. "Did you hurt yourself? Did I step on your foot and not realize it?" Damn. He thought he'd been doing so well.

She laughed. "It wasn't you. I'm working on another dance routine for a video we're doing and I overdid it this morning. I'll ice it when I get home."

"You're shooting a movie while you're doing this? That's some serious time management."

"Not a movie. A music video. We've been practicing for a couple of weeks. I think we'll get it all down in one afternoon. Ashleigh wouldn't let us do anything less. Oh, shit, sorry. Thanks for the water." Then she was gone.

Poppy had teased him on Tuesday about spending

his day off in bed, and Nick shut her down hard. She'd been shocked to hear he'd broken things off with Ashleigh but she didn't ask any questions. He didn't volunteer any answers. He knew Poppy and Ashleigh were friends so he was surprised when she let it go.

He'd returned Sandrine's text. She was sympathetic to his plight but she couldn't resist another "I told you so." He'd been halfway to her place for a commiseration drink when his brain kicked back in. Ashleigh was worse but Sandrine was still bad. He didn't want either of them in his life. Maybe it was dance instructors. They were a whole different kind of crazy than actresses.

Nick didn't want to think about it anymore. The drive home was easy, as late night traffic in LA tended to be. His problem was his bed when he got home. It was empty and smelled of dryer sheets. He'd ripped the linens off as soon as he'd gotten home on Monday and he now regretted it. No matter why Ashleigh had been in his bed, they'd had a good time there physically and mentally. She'd challenged him intellectually. Even better, they'd been sympatico on all the important stuff and hilariously opposite on the fun stuff. Even arguing with Ashleigh had been fun; at least it had been before he realized she was not only fucking him but fucking with him.

He was never going to get any rest if he started running his time with Ashleigh through his head again. He'd done that for the last two nights and hadn't slept at all. Instead, he ran through his performance over and over again, until the last time he let it go to Poppy's visit to his dressing room

One more thought popped into his head before he faded to place.

Poppy had said "we."

* * * *

If she worked hard enough, her body was too exhausted to stay awake wondering what had happened between her and Nick. Her plan succeeded for the first two days; she only stayed up for an hour obsessing about his idiocy before sleep claimed her. There was an upside to refocusing on her career instead of self-important, moron assholes. She was in the middle of a hell of a job.

Theoretically, being surrounded by sexy rock stars was the ideal distraction. The three male members of Charlie Oscar Echo provided fantasy fodder for every requirement. Bobby Wheaton, the drummer, a pale blue-eyed blond, was a sweetie. He was still a farm boy at heart and was having trouble adjusting to Los Angeles. Gregory Mills, on lead guitar and vocals, wasn't quite Ashleigh's type. He spent two years in the navy and never left it behind. With his short brown hair and brown eyes, he never lacked for company. Normally Ashleigh wouldn't be immune but recent disasters had killed any interest she might have had. Peter Blackwood was an enigma. Quietly hot, he was tall, dark, and mysterious but Ashleigh couldn't get a lock on his personality. In the same way Peter moved from guitar to keyboard to whatever else the band needed, he was friendly to everyone in his orbit while at the same time holding them at arm's length. He was a mystery a lot of women would want to solve but Ashleigh was done trying to figure out men.

Ashleigh flirted her heart out with each and every one of them. She and Poppy Travis and Caitlin Kelly rotated to the next one. Six hours later, it was all over. Eight of them, the band, the director, the cameraman, Poppy and her, huddled around the monitor. "It isn't going to get more perfect than that," Caitlin said. "I think it's time for a wrap party."

She almost said no. She wasn't in the mood to celebrate much but her friend would have none of it. "Live your life, Ash. You deserve a man who can keep up with you. Don't go home to wash your hair so you can be there in case Nick calls," Caitlin said.

"I wouldn't answer if he did, which he won't."

"Come out with us. Have a good time. I know you remember how. We have things to celebrate. Many, many celebratory things."

Caitlin was right. Ashleigh's new property wasn't the sole good thing on the horizon. The band's video was going to rock. Ashleigh's choreography was for the first song off their soon-to-be-released album. The timing was perfect since Caitlin's Olympus news was out and fans were going insane over the idea of Sean and Caitlin's characters finally getting together.

"Okay, okay. Home, change, wrap party."

Her agenda was incomplete. She did go home. She did change into a fabulous indigo micro-dress she'd picked up at a post-holiday sale. She did arrive at the Jungle. Then Caitlin called for the bar boys: Johnny, Jack, Jim, and Jose. Ashleigh flirted like mad with all of them.

Thank God Caitlin was in charge of rides home because Ashleigh was in no shape to get there on her own. The morning after nearly killed her. The hangover hurt. But it was the laughing that nearly did her in. "This is awesome. The best news report ever!" Ashleigh laughed as she held her aching head.

Caitlin didn't bother moving from her makeshift bed. "The explanation had better come with coffee."

Ashleigh flashed her phone screen. "Sandrine Gold is being sued by two different parties for fraud. I'm guessing the property owners. It couldn't happen to a nicer person."

"Glad to see you're not gloating too much. Coffee?" Caitlin begged.

Ashleigh showed mercy and delivered a cup. "Seriously, at this point how can I not laugh? I got the building I wanted and she's going to pay in all kinds of ways. Life is good."

"How about your love life?"

Ashleigh shook her head. "I liked him, Cait. The 'him' I thought he was. Why are men such assholes?"

"I don't know but they are."

"Are we talking about your anonymous non-existent non-boyfriend now?" Caitlin made a face that had taken Ashleigh years to learn. Oh, thank God for friendly distractions. "He's no longer a non-boyfriend? Who is it?" Somebody should be getting laid.

Chapter 27

Twenty-one days of performances wasn't that long. The curtain was about to rise on his twenty-fifth and final performance as Otto Blackwood and he was going to miss the character. The fictional gigolo moved from jaded cynic to cautious optimist-in-love over the course of the two hour show. Nick wished he could follow his fictional counterpart's example as efficiently.

It was more than a week later and he was still obsessing over Ashleigh. If Internet stalking had been a thing sixty-five years ago, Otto would have been all over it. Since he no longer had anyone to spend his free time with, Nick spent hours scouring Ashleigh's blog. He'd worked himself up into a self-righteous froth anticipating Ashleigh's announcement and folded like he'd been sucker punched when it appeared.

She constantly pimped her friends' successes and news. Nick didn't know why it hadn't occurred to him Ashleigh's announcement was about somebody else. He didn't believe Caitlin hesitated for a minute to give her a raving recommendation. What was worse was that it shouldn't have been a surprise. He knew about Ash's long term friendship with Caitlin Kelly and he knew about Caitlin's new regular status on Olympus; he'd been so fixated on the idea of Ashleigh setting him up he hadn't bothered looking beyond his assumptions.

"If you need your ass kicked again, I can do it for you after the show," his mother offered. "For now, keep your head in the game, Nick."

"Thanks, Mom. I can always count on you." She had gone up one side of him and down the other after his blow up with Ashleigh. Nick had been so livid he hadn't even noticed her presence. Discovering his mother had tried to make peace with his girlfriend was the icing on a shit day.

"Do you have plans after the show tonight?" his mom asked.

"I'm heading to the house. I'm not in a party mood."

"We're taking you home. We need to chat about Ashleigh. This has gone on long enough."

"I don't want to discuss it."

"Don't worry. You won't be talking. Just listening."

Nick knew she meant "home" in the traditional sense as their family's house, where Mom and Dad took care of him and straightened things out. He'd been on his own for ten years but he wasn't going to fight them. Maybe hearing from another party how bad Ashleigh was would kill the feelings he had that would not die.

His head was in the game in time for his performance. He and Poppy gave Otto and Darla their final happy-ever-after and the curtain dropped to deafening applause. "Nick, it's been a slice," Poppy said as they waited for their encore.

"It was nice what you did for Ashleigh," he said.

"It wasn't nice. It was friendship and good business. We drew the lines at the beginning of the negotiations and everybody won."

"Now you're giving me shit?"

"I'm not working with you anymore," Poppy explained. "I know you hadn't known Ashleigh for long but what about the rest of us. Me. Chris. Caitlin."

"You don't get it."

"Right. Because I'm not constantly surrounded by people who want a piece of me. Get over yourself, Nick."

So he was an asshole. That wasn't news these days.

The curtain lifted and the Ashleigh conversation

ended with her and picked up on the midnight ride to his childhood home.

"You know, you were suspicious of her, too." Nick couldn't believe his parents' hypocrisy. He and Ashleigh had been doing perfectly fine until the birthday bash from hell. Except for that thing where he'd believed Brian about Ash using his Olympus ties to get business.

Or the time where he accused her of helping herself for free advertising on the coattails of his success. Caitlin and Poppy hadn't blinked when their names went live on Ashleigh's website. In fact, they bragged about the video clips they'd provided for her.

And the time his dad said Ashleigh asked him for a job and instead of asking her about it, he nearly took her head off when she denied it, only to discover that it couldn't have been her. His mother of all people alibied her out and his father said the call came from a blocked number and hadn't really sounded like Ashleigh when he thought about it. Nick couldn't prove it but when he factored in the timing of Sandrine's text, he had a strong suspicion who made the call. After he asked, Sandrine started blocking his number.

Then there was the time when he said Ashleigh forced him to bid on a building when she had no idea what he was doing.

So maybe he fucked things up all by himself.

"You need a grand gesture," his dad suggested. "The Big Thing to win the girl back."

"I don't think one Big Thing is going to cover it. He did screw things up rather spectacularly," his mom added.

"So what do I do? Give her the testimonial I accused her of using me for and to get her lots of free publicity?"

"I thought you wanted her back. If you do that, you might as well offer her cash to get back into bed with you," his father choked out. "You want to leave money out of it."

"Then what?" Nick shouted, his exasperation overcoming his reluctance to talk about his love life with his parents. "What is it going to take?"

* * * *

Ashleigh wouldn't say the summer had flown by. The days went fast; the nights dragged on, empty and alone. The daily bouquets to her home were killing her but she kept giving them away to her neighbors. Even they were tired of them so Ashleigh had begun bringing the delicate, gorgeous, breath-taking floral art displays to the studio simply to get them out of her bedroom. She didn't need the reminder there. Instead, she was reminded each and every day at work of what she'd lost but she wasn't about to forgive him. Ashleigh prided herself on never making the same mistake twice.

She held the corner of the "Now Open" banner while Sydney fed the ring at the corner over the nail in the window frame. The studio looked amazing. Structurally it had already been in great shape. All Ashleigh had done was play with cosmetic appearances. Paint, mirrors, posters, and a little fabric. The Duncan Building studio was miles above her old one. She'd definitely made the right choice when she took the leap on the new property.

Ashleigh sent over four hundred invitations to the open house to former and returning students, friends, old classmates, and everyone else in her contacts lists. She'd also hired Rita Morales as her event photographer. The pay was crap but the exposure was good; plus, she knew from experience it never hurt to make new connections. You never knew who was going to make it big.

Her case in point walked through the door thirty seconds later, arms loaded with bags of soda and bakery boxes. "Am I late?" Caitlin asked.

"Just in time." She and Caitlin were going to do a quick routine and Caitlin agreed to stay for a couple more minutes to be gawked at and sign autographs "for a favor to be determined later." Unfortunately, it was probably her last event with the studio. With the role of Psyche becoming Caitlin's full-time gig in addition to her Charlie Oscar Echo work, Ashleigh needed to hire a new part-time instructor. But that was next week's job.

It would have been nice for the event to go flawlessly but life seldom did. Her minor calamities were limited to an unsupervised twirling competition resulting in two bumped ballerina's noggins and a sound system feedback issue which left everyone in the rehearsal area cringing. Over two hundred people cycled through the studio, getting the grand tour and offering her congratulations. The last of the guests left at nine and Ashleigh and Caitlin were left doing clean-up.

"Admit it, you're going to miss pushing a broom," Ashleigh teased.

"I'll miss my boss," Caitlin replied seriously. "Don't get me wrong. I'm thrilled we are finally breaking through but there is something to be said for friendships forged by scrambling for rent money together. It's the end of an era."

"The Ramen Years," Ashleigh quipped. "I know what you mean. I wouldn't trade them for anything but I wouldn't go back. We are all in better places now."

"What about going back a single month?"

"That would depend on the month. This last one's been good. The one before, not so much." It was almost funny how being with Nick got her through the lowest lows of her career, and he'd caused her heart to bottom out all on his own. She should have listened to her own advice and not gotten involved.

"That's going to make this awkward," Caitlin said cryptically. She took her broom and disappeared down the hall to the back storage room.

Ashleigh kept cleaning. She stashed the party supplies in her office until she had time to cart them upstairs to her new apartment. She finally got everything tucked away when she heard the stereo speakers crackle to life. "Cait, were you hanging around? Cait?"

"You know the favor that was to be repaid later? It's later," her friend called from the other room.

"Please tell me you aren't asking me to start choreography for your next video tonight," Ashleigh begged. "I'll start first thing in the morning, I swear."

"Not the favor I was talking about. Can you come out here for a moment?"

That didn't sound good.

"Ash?" a deep baritone called.

Her back stiffened at the sound of her name. The rumble in the speaker's voice hit her right in her chest, sending a tremble through her heart.

"I'm out of here. If this works out, you both owe me. If it doesn't, we're all even." Caitlin vanished out the backdoor, leaving Ashleigh alone with her number one regret.

"Nick, this is a surprise." She tried to keep her tone light and neutral and failed miserably.

"But not a pleasant one?"

She shrugged. She could barely keep a handle on her own emotions at the moment without falling apart; his feelings weren't her problem anymore. "What are you doing here? I assume Caitlin is the reason you even know where here is but why do you care?" Ashleigh knew she should be plotting revenge against her friend for setting her up but she couldn't get her brain to change tracks. It was too busy committing the sight of Nick to memory.

The bastard had the temerity to look good. Clear eyes, fresh haircut, slight five o'clock stubble that was sexy as hell. It wasn't fair. She was using two different types of foundation to cover the circles under her eyes, and drops to disguise the redness from her crying jags which were thankfully down to one or two a day.

"The place looks great. It's even nicer than the one we looked at. Did you get my flowers? And my letters?"

She had. The letters made her cry but she couldn't stop herself from reading them. He explained what had happened and why he'd behaved the way he had. It didn't change anything. She wouldn't let it. "What do you want, Nick?" Why couldn't he leave her and her broken heart in peace?

"You."

Chapter 28

Nick knew his reception was going to be cool but he didn't expect it to be quite so frigid. He thought the silence regarding his letters was bad. Every second in the room with her burned like ice. He'd screwed up relationships before, more often than he liked to think about, but this was the first time he'd ever wanted to fix what he'd broken. It killed him that it looked like he might not get the chance. Fuck him, he'd never wanted anything so much in his life.

"Why?" Ashleigh asked him. "I get that you're sorry but I'm the same person I was a month ago. I think we've established our worlds don't mesh. At all."

"I have thirty years of ingrained stupid to fight against. I didn't know you weren't playing me and by the time I realized I'd already pushed you so far away I knew you'd never come back on your own. So I came to you. I wasn't sure if you were reading my letters and I need you to know how sorry I was. I was wrong. Wrong and stupid. I am so sorry, Ash. You are the most honest person I know. Can we try again? Please?"

"What changed your mind?" Shit, she was crying now. He didn't know if that was a good thing or not. If he made it through the first part of his apology, there was an infinitesimal chance she might let him perform the second half. If that didn't convince her to take him back, he was out of ideas except for dropping to his knees and begging for another chance. He was willing to do it if he had to but he thought his current apology was more fitting.

"I did. You didn't do anything. You didn't have to. I'm the one who needed to do something and I have. I pulled my head out of my ass and saw what I lost. Please, Ash."

She was crying in earnest now. "What do you want from me, Nick?"

"I want you to dance with me."

"You don't dance."

"I do for you."

He took it as a good sign when she didn't retreat as he moved toward her. Ashleigh didn't resist when he lifted her hand to his shoulder, or when he took her other hand in his, but she didn't make any moves herself. Nick pressed the center button of the remote control Caitlin had given him and a classic rock ballad filled the room.

One, two, three. One, two, three. Nick thought about his feet but not as much as he used to. He'd contacted Caitlin after her band's video came out and had spent the last three weeks in intensive dance lessons. His butt-busting rehearsals with Ashleigh had been a walk in the park compared to what Caitlin did to him. Now he could concentrate on the feeling of having Ashleigh back in his arms, and the scent of her coconut shampoo, and of the magnificent burn of the heat of her skin against his.

"Since when can you waltz like this?"

"Since I was willing to do anything to get you back. You love to dance and I wanted to be able to give this to you. I called Caitlin and pleaded my case. She built on what you taught me." He spun her out and pulled back, this time tucking her tightly against his chest. He wasn't letting her go again.

"What's happening here?" Ashleigh whispered.

"If I'm very lucky, you're forgiving my incredible arrogance and stupidity and giving us one more chance."

There was more silence. Nick was certain his heart was cracking in his chest. Then Ashleigh relaxed in his arms, and her tense frame melted into him, her arm sliding from his shoulder to around his neck.

"I'm sorry, Ash," he whispered again. "It'll never ever happen again."

"Shut up and dance with me."

*

Nick had unquestionably screwed her over. He'd made bad choices and doubled down on them, hurting her in the process. She'd shown him the worst of her and he hadn't flinched. To discover after everything that he didn't trust her burned like acid. She understood he had to be suspicious of people in his life using him, but she'd never asked for anything from him but him. His own friends had gotten them together for fuck's sake, and he supposedly trusted them. If his own paranoia had driven them apart once, there was nothing she could do to stop it from happening again, and her heart wouldn't survive another blow like the last one he'd dealt it

But he was here, apologizing. On the other hand, they'd done this dance before. Which Nick was the real one—the ranting, thoughtless man who accused her or the humble, apologetic man in front of her? She knew her preference. From their time together, Ashleigh thought this was the real deal. This is who he was when other people weren't whispering poisonous thoughts in his ear. Or maybe, she wanted it to be.

Ashleigh took a deep breath to clear her head, and without thinking inhaled a lungful of his scent. She wanted to dive into it. It felt right to be in his arms. It felt safe but she knew the biggest danger was from the man who held her. She'd been called lots of things in her almost thirty years and most of them had been true but she'd never been a coward. Despite everything, Ashleigh still felt a connection with Nick, felt it more than ever as they waltzed around the room.

Another broken heart wouldn't kill her, as much as she might wish it would at the time. But passing up on Nick and living with the regret for the rest of her life. That might be fatal.

"We can't go back," she whispered, her cheek against his chest

"Okay."

"I don't think we can go forward from where we left off either."

Nick stopped moving. The hand around her waist convulsed painfully. "Are you saying no? Please don't say no, Ash." His voice was as rough as her emotions.

"I'm saying I think we have to start over, start fresh. Remember what happened in the past but not live in it."

Nick's chest heaved as he let out the breath he'd been holding. "So this is our first dance?"

In every way. "Yes."

"I'm glad you're going to be my last first dance, Ash. You'll never regret it."

Epilogue

Nick took no chances. He and Ashleigh had started over two months ago and he was following every single rule of dating no matter how badly it blue-balled him. He knew he and Ash took things far too fast the first time through. This time he was determined to experience and fully enjoy each step of the journey. They'd danced and dined and gone to movies and walked on the beach. And talked. Fuck, had they talked.

Ashleigh freaked about being photographed with him—she'd severely downplayed how much it bothered her when his fans went after her on the Internet. Nick went online and asked his "true" fans to lay off the special people in his life. He'd lost forty thousand followers but a majority of Ashleigh's hate mail dropped off as well so it was worth the trade.

He'd discussed his exes and the various things they'd demanded of him. As a result, Ashleigh kept him informed of her upcoming advertising and special events to ensure he knew when he might be walking into something when he showed up at the studio to visit her. It was good she sent him constant updates; the studio had taken off at the new location. He didn't mind the occasional "OMG, it's Nick Thurston!" but he managed to avoid the worst of it. A couple of private students didn't even freak out at him anymore when he arrived before the end of their classes.

Her new place was a lot more spacious than her last apartment too. Since she'd bought the building including the three apartments on the second floor, as landlord, Ashleigh claimed the double sized one for herself. She rented one to a friend of a friend who Nick hadn't met, and the other was currently empty as the old tenant had recently vacated.

That's where they were after their third date to Disneyland. She slipped her hands under the lapels of his jacket again. "I'm going to invite you upstairs. Are you going to turn me down again?"

"Are you sure? We can wait if you're not sure." His dick was going to kill him. Almost a month of being without Ashleigh, and two more of being near enough to do anything but be inside her left him a quivering wreck at the end of their dates but it had been for a good cause. They knew each other this time. The trust they'd assumed was real now.

"I'm sure."

It was going to make whatever came next even sweeter.

The End

About Elle Rush

Elle Rush is a Canadian romance author from Winnipeg, Manitoba. When she's not travelling, she's hard at work writing her contemporary romance eBooks which are set all over the world. Elle earned a degree in Spanish and French, barely passed German, and is starting to learn Italian and Filipino. She has flunked poetry in every language she's ever taken. She also has mild addictions to tea, cookbooks and the sci-fi channel. Follow her at www.ellerush.com or on Pinterest, Facebook and Twitter, and keep up with her free newsletter.

Other Books

Hollywood to Olympus

1. Screen Idol
2. Drama Queen
3. Leading Man
4. It Girl (coming soon)

Publisher's Note

Please help this author's career by posting an honest review wherever you purchased this book.